Bridgett tried not to stare at the man who'd just entered the luncheonette.

"Welcome to The Magpie," she said, reminding herself to breathe.

He was definitely easy on the eyes—*gorgeous brown eyes*—almost familiar in a way, but she was positive she hadn't seen him before.

"How may I service you today?"

Please tell me I did not say that!

Mortified, Bridgett closed her eyes and vainly struggled to keep a nervous laugh of embarrassment in check. She failed. "Let me try this again."

"It's okay," he drawled. "I'm intrigued by your offer."

If she'd thought his eyes were gorgeous before, they were downright intoxicating up close. And his voice reminded her of a song, but she couldn't place which one. She needed a distraction, and this sexy newcomer had just claimed top billing.

Dear Reader,

Ever since I wrote *Betting on Texas*, the first book in the Welcome to Ramblewood series, I've wanted to give Bridgett Jameson her own book. The Magpie waitress is one of those small-town girls who has never been much past the town's border. She refuses to settle for the average cowboy and figures she'll recognize "the one" when she sees him. But who? I asked myself that question for over a year.

After an online chat with fellow Harlequin author, Sarah M. Anderson, I knew exactly who Mr. Right would be. Our late night Twitter banter sparked the idea for *Back to Texas*. Mix one country girl with a rebel newcomer who's hiding from his notorious past and there's bound to be some Texas-sized trouble.

Adam Steele is a departure from my usual cowboy heroes, but he quickly grew to become one of my favorites. Everyone has their own story to tell and often those stories are full of regrets. Adam certainly has a mile-long list of them. While life doesn't allow for do-overs, sometimes all it takes is the kindness of strangers for us to begin again.

Feel free to stop in and visit me at amandarenee.com. I'd love to hear from you. Happy reading!

Amanda Renee

BACK TO TEXAS

—

AMANDA RENEE

◆ **HARLEQUIN**® AMERICAN ROMANCE®

Recycling programs
for this product may
not exist in your area.

ISBN-13: 978-0-373-75569-1

Back to Texas

Copyright © 2015 by Amanda Renee

Printed in U.S.A.

www.Harlequin.com

Amanda Renee was raised in the northeast and now wriggles her toes in the warm sand of coastal South Carolina. She was discovered through Harlequin's So You Think You Can Write contest and began writing for the American Romance line. When not creating stories about love, laughter and things that go bump in the night, she enjoys the company of her schnoodle, Duffy, photography, playing guitar and anything involving horses. You can visit her at amandarenee.com.

Books by Amanda Renee

HARLEQUIN AMERICAN ROMANCE

Welcome to Ramblewood

Betting on Texas

Home to the Cowboy

Blame It on the Rodeo

A Texan for Hire

Visit the Author Profile page
at Harlequin.com for more titles.

Chapter One

"Who do you think should play us in the movie?"

"Do actresses even come in your size?" Waitress Bridgett Jameson poured her newfound sister, Abby Winchester, another cup of coffee. She drummed her fingers on the luncheonette counter waiting for her next order. This wasn't a conversation Bridgett wanted to have so early in the morning—let alone smack dab in the middle of The Magpie, where every word you said spread across town faster than a sneeze through a screen door.

Abby pouted. "What I lack in stature, I compensate for in charm."

Lack in stature. The nine-inch height difference between them made their recent discovery even more shocking. Fraternal twins. Bridgett didn't think she'd ever get used to the idea.

She grabbed a rag and wiped the counter, hoping someone would come to her rescue. She didn't dislike Abby. It was the situation she hated. A month ago, they'd been well on their way to becoming good friends. Maybe they'd have a chance at it again once Bridgett absorbed the fact that her mother had lied to her for the past twenty-eight years. And the revelation that her biological father was the town's mayor, Darren Fox. A man she'd seen almost every day of her life, but who had never acknowledged her existence. Heck, he didn't even leave her a decent tip.

Gutted by the lies private investigator Clay Tanner had unearthed regarding her and Abby's parentage two weeks ago, Bridgett was uncertain what she should do next. Up until then, she'd had a rather normal life in her hometown of Ramblewood, Texas. The people she worked with at the luncheonette, along with her friends and mother, had collectively formed the only family Bridgett had ever known, and it'd suited her just fine. Of course, she'd fantasized about who her father was. Who wouldn't? Especially after the way her mother had glamourized him.

Her mother had claimed Bridgett was the product of a love affair, and that Bridgett's father had been an Air Force pilot who had transferred overseas before Ruby had known she was pregnant. Never to be heard from again. Well, she was half right. Bridgett was the result of an affair. And Darren *had* been in the Air Force. But that was where the truth had ended and twenty-eight years of lies had begun.

"Why would anyone want to make a movie about us?" Bridgett stole a quick glance at the kitchen passthrough window once more for her order.

"All the crap we've just been through has amazing movie-of-the-week potential." Abby removed a bundle of magazines and notes from her bag, fanning them across the counter. "Please help me plan this wedding. New Year's Eve is in a few months. If Clay has his way, we'll be married in the barn with a beer-and-pretzel main course."

The private investigator hadn't merely discovered she and Abby were sisters, he'd officially become Abby's fiancé last week. In the span of seven days, the two of them had gotten engaged, packed up what Abby needed from the house she'd shared with her brother in South Carolina and moved her across the country to Clay's ranch.

"Between working here and at the Bed & Biscuit, I don't see where I'd have the time."

"But you have to." Abby reached for Bridgett's hand, her smile desperate, almost pleading. Bridgett suspected her sister was on the verge of asking her *the question.* The one Bridgett had hoped to avoid. At the very least, she hadn't wanted it to be a public event where the neighborhood busybodies listened in on their conversation. "I'm hoping you'll be my maid of honor," Abby said.

Bridgett stared down at the all-too-personal contact, recognizing that if she moved away she'd offend Abby. "I'm flattered, but we're virtually strangers. I'd think one of your friends would appreciate the honor."

"Sure, yeah, you're right." Abby withdrew her hand, returning her attention to the magazines. "One of my friends—no problem."

So much for trying to spare her feelings.

Abby dropped her eyes and rapidly thumbed through the pages. To say their lives had changed overnight was an understatement. On top of the twin-sister revelation,

Darren had suddenly grown a conscience and had decided he wanted a relationship with his daughters. He could wait an eternity for all she cared. The likelihood of a reunion was zilch. Bridgett found it impossible to face the man who'd demanded her mother to get *rid of her* before she'd been born. At that time, Darren had known of only one baby. The birth of twins had been a surprise to them both.

Bridgett cut Abby a slice of rum vanilla cream pie as a peace offering and set it next to her coffee. While the truth may have been hard for Bridgett to accept, she'd known who her mother was all along. When Abby had learned her parents had adopted her, she'd been rightfully outraged.

Ruby's reasons for separating her twin daughters disgusted Bridgett. Not knowing she even carried twins, Ruby had decided to give her baby up for adoption months earlier. When Abby was born, Ruby had refused to hold her, banning the infant from the room. She had already promised to give Abby to a couple in town—Darren's Air Force buddy and his wife. When Bridgett had unexpectedly arrived a half hour later, Ruby had believed it was a sign to keep the second baby.

Abby sliced her fork through the pie's tip and took a bite, appearing to savor the mouthful. "I think this became my favorite dessert the first time I ate here. Thank you."

"You're welcome." Bridgett grabbed the almost-full sugar dispenser in front of Abby and topped it up. Afraid her thoughts would betray her, she pretended to be busy.

Bridgett had mixed emotions about Abby. She'd always wanted a sister, but Abby's arrival had unearthed a mountain of drama. Ramblewood, Texas, might be a tiny dot on the map, but when Darren's paternity secret had surfaced the day before he'd announced his much-anticipated run for senate, their unsuspecting Hill Country town had become quite the spectacle. Complete with constant media coverage. If one more person asked her for an interview or snapped her photo, she'd scream. Luckily, it had begun to die down over the past two days when Darren had renounced his senate run. It still hadn't quelled the local gossip, though.

Ruby's lies had compounded from the day of the twins' births. The extent of the deception sickened Bridgett. Ruby had claimed she and the twins' grandparents had had a major falling out when she'd told them she was pregnant. Ruby maintained to this day that she had no idea where they lived. Bridgett wondered if the story was true or another fabrication. Their grandparents would probably be easy to locate, especially since Abby was engaged to a private investigator. But since they'd never tried to contact Bridgett, she had no desire to search for them.

Growing up, Bridgett had suspected Ruby was keeping secrets based on the quick way her mother had dismissed any questions she'd had regarding her grandparents or the name of her father. Eventually, Bridgett had given up and stopped asking.

Now Bridgett just wished people's tongues would stop wagging long enough for her to regain her footing. The media coverage had turned her and Abby into local celebrities. It irritated Bridgett how the reporters always found the need to mention their ages along with the fact that Bridgett was single. Since the news broke it seemed as if every bachelor within a ten-mile radius had asked her for a date. She didn't need any coddling and she certainly didn't need any extra baggage in her life. Besides, she refused to settle for just anybody.

"Order up," Bert called through the pass-through window, giving Bridgett the opening to walk away from the increasingly uncomfortable conversation with her sister. *Her sister.* Bridgett doubted she'd get used to those words anytime soon. She used to take waking up in a good mood for granted. Now she prayed for a normal day. No stares or whispers. No tearful phone calls from her mother. Normal was miles away from Ramblewood and she'd rather be anywhere but here. And hopefully that day would come sooner than later.

Bridgett refused to leave anything else to chance. Every afternoon she made of point of checking the Help Wanted ads online in the towns at least a hundred miles from Ramblewood. She'd jump at the first offer. For now, she kept her plans to herself, not wanting to risk anyone trying to talk her out of it. She wanted to secure a job before she left town. Her ultimate goal was to open her own restaurant, but until she found one she could afford, she'd make do managing someone else's.

Bridgett grabbed the plates and headed for her customer's table at the front of the luncheonette. When she passed Lark she whispered, "Take over counter duty for me." The other waitress nodded.

Bridgett had been hesitant when Maggie Dalton, The

Magpie's owner, had hired Lark Meadow a few weeks earlier. Lark had rolled into Ramblewood on the bus. Disheveled, with not much more than a duffel bag and a guitar, Lark had said she was on her way to New Mexico after a disastrous string of Nashville auditions. She'd sold everything she had owned to take a gamble on her big dream and no longer had a home to go back to. Refusing to turn the woman away, Maggie had helped Lark rent a studio apartment above the florist's shop across the street.

Bridgett had a hunch the newcomer was on the run, but if Maggie wasn't concerned, she wouldn't pry, either. Lark seemed to appreciate the privacy and she'd turned out to be a welcome addition to The Magpie. Considering Bridgett planned to leave town soon, she felt less guilty knowing another waitress was already trained and in place.

Bridgett took a few more orders before she noticed Abby packing up her wedding explosion. The normally perky pint-size blonde's shoulders slumped as she mumbled a quick "see you later" on the way out. Bridgett sighed, wishing she hadn't been so abrupt with her sister. If only Abby hadn't asked her to stand up for her at the wedding.

Bridgett wanted to get to know Abby on her own terms, but Abby was relentless. She stopped in the luncheonette every morning for breakfast, called at night to share what she'd learned at her new job and sometimes she showed up at the Bed & Biscuit uninvited. It was too much, too soon.

Through the vinyl magpie-bird cutouts on the luncheonette's picture window, Bridgett watched Abby trudge to her car and drive away. She hated hurting Abby, but Bridgett wasn't ready to embrace the happy family-unit idea yet.

"May I have a refill, dear?" Charlotte Hargrove, one of Ramblewood's biggest gossips, waved her cup in the air. Bridgett removed the coffee carafe from the brewer and wondered how long it would take before her mother called and demanded she be nicer to Abby. Twenty minutes was the norm for Charlotte's gossip to spread, but it had been known to travel faster than a bee-stung stallion when it was particularly juicy.

"Are things okay between you two?" Charlotte asked when Bridgett arrived with the coffee.

Hesitating, Bridgett tried to figure out how to answer the question without feeding into the rumor mill. "Abby's a bit overwhelmed with the wedding plans."

"Won't she be a beautiful bride?" The older woman's round cheeks brightened when she spoke. "Tiny as she is she'd probably pass for a cake topper in her gown. I do hope they start a family soon. I bet they'll have the most darling children."

And *there* was the knife twist. Charlotte wasn't a fool. She knew Bridgett wanted kids. Growing up, Bridgett had longed for a big family, begging her mother to marry and have more children. Ruby had delighted in her daughter's dreams and shared them with her clients. Because of her mother's well-intentioned meddling, half the town seemed determined to set Bridgett up on one embarrassing blind date after another.

After many failed attempts and a few short-term romances, Bridgett had learned to say no to any further matchmaking. So she hadn't found *the one*. She refused to settle. What was the rush anyway? Although, she did have to admit, it had smarted when her sister had blown into town and snagged herself a husband. Not that Bridgett had been interested in Clay. She never went for the strong silent types. But he and Abby suited each other perfectly.

Bridgett totaled Charlotte's bill and left it upside down on the table. "They'll have beautiful children. Enjoy the rest of your day."

Hoping for a mental break, Bridgett headed into the kitchen. From his position at the grill, Bert briefly glanced her way. No one worried about their beloved, yet rough-around-the-edges cook asking too many questions. Bert kept mostly to himself.

"Do you need any help?" Bridgett asked. The breakfast rush had wound down and she'd had enough of the remaining customers' endless stares. They acted as though she'd break at any moment.

"I'm good." Bert plated a stack of pancakes and set them on the pass-through. "Lark, table four." He smacked the silver service bell.

"I'll take it out." Since she'd asked Lark to cover the counter, Bridgett could manage delivering one of her orders. Besides, Charlotte was on her way out.

Bridgett had begun waitressing at sixteen and twelve years later here she remained. The Magpie wasn't exactly her career choice. She enjoyed her job to a certain degree, but she'd meant for it to be a stepping-stone to owning her own place. When Bridgett was nine, she'd stumbled across a weathered Betty Crocker cookbook at a yard sale. Her mother couldn't cook to feed an ant, so Bridgett had begun preparing their meals out of necessity. Cooking for two had been fine at first, but the more Bridgett experimented with different spices, the more she wanted to share her creations with someone other than her mother. Maggie gave her kitchen time when they were slow. A few of her recipes had been house specials, and her Mexican *cemita* sandwich filled with pork, avocado, cheese and chili had become a regular menu item. When Maggie had converted the upstairs offices into a second kitchen, she'd asked Bridgett to be her sous-chef during catering events. It allowed her more cooking time and the extra money she made went into her restaurant fund.

Bridgett delivered Lark's order and started another pot of coffee. Life wasn't perfect, but whose ever was? Bridgett had been reasonably happy up until recent events, and although she still kept an eye out for Mr. Right, it wasn't a priority. She had enjoyed her quiet, unassuming existence until she'd headlined the evening news. She'd contemplated dipping into her savings account and leaving town immediately, but her restaurant dream was the one thing that kept her going on most days. Until she could find a better solution, she'd opted to move out of her mother's house.

When her friend Mazie had offered Bridgett a room at the Bed & Biscuit, she couldn't have packed fast enough. She needed to break away from the one person she'd never imagined would betray her. Of course, Mazie had given her a room rent-free, but Bridgett refused to be a charity case. Bridgett assisted Mazie in the kitchen and cleaned the inn to repay her friend's generous hospitality.

Bridgett thought she had made it clear she wanted—scratch that—*needed* time to think, but very few people seemed to listen. She was confused by the truth and hurt by the lies. Surely a little breathing room wasn't too much to ask for.

Bridgett clipped another ticket to the order wheel and spun it to Bert. He and Maggie may have taught her how to run a restaurant, but Mazie instructed her on the finer cooking techniques she had learned at Le Cordon Bleu in Paris. Bridgett studiously took notes and added each lesson to her own overstuffed *dream book*.

Unlike most of her friends, Bridgett hadn't had the desire to go to school to learn a trade or earn a degree. She preferred the hands-on approach. That was the lie she told herself anyway. She couldn't afford to go to school then or now. Darren had managed to send all three of his legitimate children to Ivy League schools. Abby's parents had sent her to college—seven years' worth for her to become a physical therapist. Out of Darren's five children, Bridgett was the only one without a career or college degree. Her jaw tightened. Jealousy wouldn't solve anything. She had the strength and determination to make it on her own. And she would make it, too. Someday.

Bridgett bussed a table, mentally envisioning the floor plan of her own restaurant. As she nudged the kitchen door with her hip, the bells above the entrance jingled.

"Welcome to The Magpie." Halfway through the door to the kitchen, Bridgett caught a glimpse of the man standing just inside the luncheonette's entrance. The plates precariously balanced on her arms began to slip. He smiled at her. "Oh, my stars," she whispered, struggling to prevent the stack from crashing to the floor.

Quickly depositing the dishes in the kitchen, she ducked down and made her way to the pass-through to sneak a peek at the man without appearing too obvious.

"What on earth are you doing?" Bert asked from the grill.

Bridgett shushed him and attempted another glimpse. The man was definitely easy on the eyes—*gorgeous brown eyes*—almost familiar in a way, but she was positive she hadn't seen him before.

Crap. Lark greeted him and led him to the counter. Bridgett crouch-walked to the door, stood and took a deep breath.

"He's just a man, sweetheart," Bert chuckled as he plated another order. "Don't get yourself in a state. Go on out there and act natural."

Since when did Bert give relationship advice?

Bridgett couldn't bear to turn around and see the expression on the cook's face. Shoulders squared, she casually entered the dining area and strolled behind the counter.

"Thanks for your assistance before, Lark." Bridgett touched the woman's shoulder. "I've got this.

"How may I service you today?"

Please tell me I did not say that!

Mortified, Bridgett closed her eyes and vainly struggled to keep a nervous laugh in check. She failed. "Let me try this again."

"It's okay," he drawled. "I'm intrigued by your offer."

If she'd thought his eyes were gorgeous before, they were downright intoxicating up close. And his voice reminded her of a song, but she couldn't place which one. She needed a distraction, and this sexy newcomer had just claimed top billing.

ADAM STEELE HADN'T eaten since yesterday—a day he'd rather forget. When he'd arrived at his sister's in a sorry state, she'd taken him in. She'd cut and colored his hair from bleached blond to its natural brown, then forced him to shave off his jet-black beard. The new Adam was unrecognizable, even to himself.

"Are you in town for this weekend's Harvest Festival?" the waitress asked. The name *Bridgett* was embroidered on the front of her pink-and-white fifties-style uniform, next to where the zipper began to reveal a hint of cleavage. Normally he'd pass on the whole retro vibe, but it worked on her.

"The festival's a pretty big deal here, huh?" The main reason he'd pulled into town had been his growling stomach. He also wanted to test out his new look to see if anyone would recognize him. Bodyguards usually accompanied him and his band when they traveled. Outside of the quick shopping spree he and his sister had made to buy some normal clothes for his trip, this was his first solo performance and he needed to be sure he'd be able to travel incognito. How ironic his "disguise" was his real identity.

Bridgett's eyes widened and Adam feared he'd already blown his cover. "You're not a reporter, are you?" She took a step back. "Because I've had my fill of those lately."

Adam inwardly cringed. "A reporter? People have called me many things, but a reporter hasn't been one of them. Why would I be?"

"Because you answered my question with a question. It's what they do. And I've endured enough questions to last forever."

Okay, retro girl has a problem with reporters. After countless world tours and the tabloids' constant fabrications about him and his band, they ranked at the bottom of Adam's list also.

"No, I'm not a reporter or remotely connected to journalism. What do they want with you?"

"Corrupt mayor, political scandal." Bridgett quickly broke eye contact, reached into her apron pocket and removed her order pad. "Sorry, I shouldn't have assumed."

"The sign for the festival caught my attention and I thought I'd check it out. Can you recommend a hotel?"

"New to the area? I haven't seen you in here before."

"I'm from Katy. Three hours to the east." Adam almost flinched at his own answer. When had he last told the truth regarding his hometown? Nine, or, ten years ago—maybe. After that long, he hadn't expected it to roll off his tongue so easily. Tension usually surrounded the question. This morning it was absent. The fear someone would expose his lie vanished with the truth. If anyone had recognized his "true" identity in the past, his credibility in the industry would have ended.

He'd managed to keep the truth from everyone, including his band. The world knew him as The Snake. It was the biographical lie his first manager had created and he'd never been able to escape it. An extremely lucrative persona had grown from that lie, playing on people's emotions. The orphaned street kid from one of Miami's roughest neighborhoods, discovered on a corner playing guitar. Only it wasn't true.

It wasn't until this last tour when he'd finally came clean with his drummer, Phil, telling his best friend how he actually hailed from Texas. Strangely enough, the story hadn't surprised Phil. Bogus childhoods weren't unusual in Los Angeles. But most people hadn't gone to the extremes Adam had. He'd created a career based upon that lie. If the truth surfaced, Adam knew he'd lose all credibility in the music industry. The products he currently endorsed would take a hit, as well. Why would anyone want to be associated with a man who had not only lied to the world, but also shunned his family in order to make millions of dollars?

"We don't have much in the center of town, except for the Bed & Biscuit—biscuit as in dog biscuit. Mazie, the owner, caters to people with pets, although oddly enough she doesn't own one herself. But her sister, Lexi, is an equine veterinarian and… Good heavens, I'm rambling."

Adam enjoyed the pink tinge flooding Bridgett's cheeks. Her high ponytail enhanced her long, slender neck. He'd love to loosen those thick honey-red waves and watch them fall down around her shoulders.

Adam caught himself staring at her, neither one of

them making a move to speak. *Form words, Adam.
You're no stranger to women.* He had certainly par-
taken in his fair share of the opposite sex in his younger
days, but none of them had caused his heart to beat like
a revolutionary war drum.

"Bridgett!" A voice boomed from the kitchen. "For
the third time, order up, table seven."

"Huh?" Bridgett shook her head and Adam wondered if she'd figured out who he was. "I need to— I'll
be— I—"

"She'll be with you in a minute. Meanwhile, you
can look *this* over." The other waitress thrust a menu at
him, placed her hands on both of Bridgett's shoulders
and turned her toward the pass-through window. Adam
couldn't hear everything the other woman whispered to
Bridgett, but he clearly understood the words, "What
the heck is wrong with you?"

Bridgett swatted the woman away when she offered
to take his order instead. He'd had women stumble over
him before, but this was different. He genuinely didn't
think they knew him from…well…Adam.

"I'm sorry." She returned, her voice interrupting his
thoughts. "Let's start from the beginning. I'm Bridgett,
welcome to Ramblewood."

She offered her hand. Her skin felt soft as velvet
against his callused fingers. Adam wondered if his attraction to her was real or if the sudden freedom to
roam where he wished had seduced him. He probably
had a ridiculous grin plastered across his face, but he
didn't care.

"Adam. It's a pleasure to meet you. Do you mind if

I ask you a question?" Not waiting for her answer, he rose slightly on his stool and leaned on the counter, her hand still in his. "Are the boysenberries really local in the Local Boysenberry French Toast?"

Bridgett moved closer to him and whispered, "Yes, and it's to die for...my personal favorite."

"Well, on that recommendation—"

The sound of a woman clearing her throat caused them both to look down the counter. The other waitress stood with both arms full of dirty dishes, one eyebrow raised.

Releasing him, Bridgett stood up straight and adjusted her apron. "And this is Lark."

"Charmed," Lark grumbled. "Unless you want more gossip floating around, I suggest you two cool it until you find a more private place to ogle each other."

"More gossip? Involving you?" Adam asked. Could there be more to the reporter story than Bridgett indicated earlier?

"She means small-town gossip in general." Bridgett may have dismissed the question, but Adam caught the slightly aggravated inflection in her voice. The sidelong glance she shot Lark was a clear message for the other woman to shut up. "Where were we? Oh, yes, the French toast. A local farmer grows and cold-pack cans the boysenberries so we have them year-round. Maggie's boysenberry syrup is incredible. And a few of our pastries have a boysenberry filling."

"Maggie?"

"Maggie Dalton." Bridgett checked her watch. "She

owns the luncheonette, but she ran to the farmers' market this morning. She should return any minute."

Bridgett's green eyes reminded him of the dew-covered clover he'd seen in Ireland last summer. "I'll have an order with a side of bacon and a coffee."

"Coming right up."

Bridgett bounced into the kitchen, her ponytail swinging. Adam swiveled on his stool, checking out the rest of the luncheonette. The complete opposite of the clubs and expensive restaurants he usually frequented. Only a dozen tables and booths filled the narrow space. He'd once enjoyed eating in similar places. Comfortable and cozy. Where everyone knew everyone else. He hadn't realized how much he'd missed those simpler days until now. He'd trade every cent he'd made to have his family back.

The vibration of his cell pulsed in his leather jacket. He tugged it out of the pocket, powered the phone off and tossed it on the counter. Twenty-four hours ago, Adam had knocked on his parents' door and pleaded for forgiveness. He probably would have gotten further with them if he hadn't reeked of whiskey and stale cigarettes. The final night of a tour meant an enormous party for the band and crew. In the spirit of the celebration, Adam had drunk more than he should have. He'd celebrated for a different reason…his final show. Period. He'd decided to quit when another fight had broken out between the bass guitarist and drummer minutes before hitting the stage. Tempers and egos had reached a boiling point and they hadn't discussed future projects in ages.

As the band's front man, Adam knew he needed to

let them and their management in on his decision. But he'd rather do it in person. He'd bailed early on last night's party. Houston had been their final concert—an hour away from his hometown. The fact that he had to be assisted by the limo driver to climb out of the car should have been his sign to wait another day or two. But he couldn't wait. He had wanted to share his decision with his parents first. When he'd rung their bell at four in the morning, his mother had appeared in the sidelight window next to the door. She hadn't recognized him until he'd shouted, "Mom, it's me" loud enough for her to hear. Adam had placed his palm on the glass. Slowly she'd lifted hers, matching his on the other side of the window. She'd held his gaze. The longing and loss etched into her face had broken his heart. Squeezing her eyes shut, she'd mouthed his name and disappeared from view.

He had repeatedly rung the bell, calling to her. He'd stopped when he heard the deadbolt unlock. His father had swung the door wide, stormed onto the portico and demanded that Adam leave before someone overheard him and called the police. He'd thrown in a "have you looked at yourself in the mirror" followed by the crushing blow "you're no longer a part of this family." When Adam had tried to explain he wanted to move home to Katy, his father had cut him short, reiterating that he needed to leave.

Adam's jaw clenched at the memory. When he'd arrived at his sister Lizzy's, she'd been waiting for him, tipped off by their parents. She'd had no choice but to let him in since he owned the house she lived in. Adam had purchased it two years ago, after Lizzy's ex-husband had beaten the crap out of her. The home was tucked away in a gated community boasting its own security guards. Adam had added an alarm system rivaling Fort Knox to ensure her safety.

It had irked his parents how he'd provided for Lizzy. Especially when they'd offered her a place to live on their small ranch. Her violent marriage and the traumatic end to her career because of those injuries had almost been too much for Lizzy to bear. Moving in with their parents would have been the final blow to Lizzy's pride. And although Adam had arranged for a generous bank account for Lizzy to draw on if she needed, she hadn't touched a dime of his money.

He'd still been dressed in his fetid stage leathers, and Lizzy had demanded he shower before she'd permitted him to sit on any of the furniture. She had thrown his clothes in the trash can outside and had given him a pair of sweats and a T-shirt her new boyfriend had kept at the house. Determined to convince his family he wasn't the terrible person they'd presumed he was, Adam had asked his sister to transform him physically into someone more socially acceptable.

Lizzy may not have approved of his choices, but she'd stood by him when no one else had. She'd offered to explain Adam's decision to their parents while he wrapped up things in Los Angeles. He dreaded the fallout from management and his fans. But if he wanted his family to take him seriously, he needed to make real changes and put an end to the lies.

"Cream and sugar?" Bridgett interrupted his thoughts.

Adam swiveled to face the counter. "Yes, thank you. I guess I'll need a dog to stay at the Biscuit Shack. Have one I can borrow?"

"Bed & Biscuit." The corners of her mouth lifted. "The Biscuit Shack's on Highway 87 in Boerne—great food. It wouldn't matter even if you had a dog because it's booked solid this weekend."

"Order up." Bert called from the kitchen.

Bridgett set the breakfast platter in front of Adam, along with a small stainless steel pitcher of boysenberry syrup. He poured it over the berry-filled toast. Bridgett propped an elbow on the counter, waiting for him to take the first bite. Normally he'd have been self-conscious of someone watching him eat, but the aroma of warmed berries and bacon beckoned. He lifted the fork to his mouth and winked at Bridgett. Then the euphoria set in.

"This is the best French toast I've ever had." And he'd tried various countries' versions of it throughout his travels. Adam closed his eyes and savored another bite. "It's incredible. Put in another order for me, because one won't be enough."

Bridgett slipped a pad from her pocket and wrote another ticket. "Just don't make yourself sick," she cautioned. "I'll put it in now. I have to check on my other customers, but I'll be back."

Adam ate the rest of his meal, reveling in his anonymity. He could adjust to this. The physical and mental exhaustion from traipsing the globe for almost a decade had left him craving a simpler existence. Ramblewood may not have been a planned stop, but he needed a vacation from stardom and a chance to regroup before he announced to the world that his life had been one giant lie. Besides, no one would think to search for him in the sleepy Texas town.

He'd have to be careful not to get too close to the beautiful waitress, though. There was no sense pulling an unsuspecting person into the mess his life had become, especially if she was trying to avoid the media.

Chapter Two

"I can't remember when I last saw a smile on your face."
After her shift at the luncheonette, Bridgett had bee-
lined for the inn. Mazie stopped chopping onions long
enough to contemplate the favor being asked of her. "If
Adam is responsible for it, I guess there's no harm in
him staying here."

Bridgett flattened her lips, sucking them inward to
hide the goofy smile threatening to expose her excitement. "Thank you, Mazie."

She fought the urge to hug her friend. Heck, she
barely believed she'd had the grit to ask that Mazie rent
Adam the room reserved for out-of-town family. She
still hadn't figured out what had prompted her to be so
brazen, especially since the room was just down the
hall from hers. That thought alone caused her stomach
to do a few somersaults.

Although the town of Katy was three hours away, it
was still close enough for them to see each other again
after the Harvest Festival. If he wanted to. Why it even
mattered baffled her. She hadn't planned to stick around

town much longer herself. Then again, maybe she'd add Katy to her job-search locations.

Mazie's smile tightened before she returned her attention to the chopping board. "Please be careful. You've been through quite a bit and I don't want to see you jump at the first guy you meet as a way to forget what's happened. Whether this man's here or not, you still need to deal with your family."

"My eyes are wide open." Bridgett grabbed a fallen dish towel from the floor and tossed it onto the counter. "He needs a room for the weekend and I've no intention of running away with him. Although, who'd blame me for wanting to ditch this town."

Mazie stilled her knife, looking at Bridgett. "You and I have watched out for each other since the day we first met in pre-school. I wouldn't be much of a friend if I didn't say your interest in this man worries me. There are plenty of hotels with vacancies outside of Ramblewood."

"Please don't feel obligated." Bridgett poked her head out of the kitchen wanting to ensure Adam hadn't wandered in and overheard their conversation. "If you're uncomfortable with him staying here, I understand."

Mazie added the onions to a large, blue-and-white speckled enameled pan. "We're having roasted ratatouille and goat-cheese-stuffed crepes tonight. I'll set an extra place at the table for Adam."

Bridgett couldn't help grinning, and her body tingled in anticipation. With Adam staying down the hall from her, maybe they'd be able to spend some time together.

"Well don't stand here." Mazie waved her away. "He's waiting outside, isn't he?"

Bridgett blinked rapidly. "Oh. Right." She spun to leave. "Thanks again, Mazie."

"And don't run off to Vegas and get yourself hitched." Mazie still held a tiny grudge against her sister for eloping last year, although she'd never admit it aloud. Lexi's elopement had stunned Mazie, along with the rest of Ramblewood. But it hadn't compared to the snub she'd felt when she'd found out Lexi had asked Bridgett to be the maid of honor. It had been a spur-of-the-moment decision—Lexi hadn't meant to hurt her sister.

Bridgett tried to tamp down her excitement as she walked to the front porch, where she'd asked Adam to wait. She may be desperate for a distraction, but she wasn't desperate for a man. She pushed open the screen door. "Adam, I—" Where was he? And where was his truck? He'd parked it at the curb in front of the Bed & Biscuit earlier.

Disappointment tore through Bridgett. Heaviness in her chest replaced the tingling sensation she'd experienced moments earlier. She had permitted herself a small piece of happiness and as quickly as it'd come, it had vanished.

A voice called out to her when she headed inside. "I asked him to move." Bridgett turned toward the street. One of Ramblewood's men in blue stood on the other side of the front gate. "The weather's supposed to remain nice tonight and the festival vendors decided to set up early. His truck was in the way, so I asked him to move it to the side lot."

Bridgett let out a huge breath and sagged against the porch railing. She had no right to feel relief, disappointment or any emotion for a man she'd met hours ago. Not for a stranger passing through town. Mazie's words echoed through her head. Bridgett's first instinct had been to take a gamble on a new life and love, just as her sister had. Abby had managed to snag a fiancé, find her dream job and move half way across the country in under a month. If she had the opportunity to begin again in a new town, she'd jump at it. One way or another, she needed out of Ramblewood. And who knew, maybe after getting to know a little more about Adam, Bridgett would be glad he was moving on. Or, maybe she'd want more...

"Thank you." Bridgett waved goodbye to the officer and straightened some of the potted flowers along the porch. She'd waited patiently for Mr. Right. Of course, it was too soon to know where Adam fit into the mix. When Bridgett experimented with a new dish, she tried different ingredients to test how they tasted together. Sometimes she had a hit, other times a flop. Relationships weren't any different. Bridgett had stopped dating after her last boyfriend, not wanting to risk another disappointment. But Adam was a new ingredient in Ramblewood. And she welcomed the opportunity to explore the possibilities.

ADAM POCKETED HIS keys as he approached the inn's front porch. Unnoticed, he watched Bridgett rearrange various fall plants. His mother would be able to rattle off every plant's common name along with its genus and species. To him, they were just puffy flowers. Mums possibly, but he couldn't be certain. His mother had a passion for horticulture, but she'd never treated it as more than a hobby. Adam had once promised his mother he would build her a huge nursery so she could run the business she'd always envisioned. She'd laughed off the prospect and Adam knew she hadn't taken him seriously. When he'd stumbled upon the sketches she'd tucked away in a drawer, he'd vowed to make her dreams a reality. And he would have, except for one problem. By the time he'd acquired the financial security to give his parents anything they desired, they'd already disowned him.

It wasn't just his band's notoriety for destroying hotel rooms or the leaked cell-phone photos of him with a certain centerfold. Adam hung his head as he remembered the time he had attempted to explain the pictures to his family. The groupies appalled his mother, although Dad had once hinted that he was a bit jealous of his son. Lizzy said his parents had questioned the tabloid rumors about his supposed drug addiction and a reported sex tape, and even if they had been true, they might have moved past it. When he didn't fly home after Lizzy's ex put her in the hospital or when his father had a heart attack, he'd sealed his own fate.

Adam's gut clenched at the thought. It shouldn't have mattered where he was touring. He could have postponed the shows…but he hadn't. With that, and the way he'd misrepresented his upbringing, refusing to acknowledge their existence, he couldn't blame them for disowning him.

The Snake's persona claimed he had bounced from one foster home to another, barely remembering his mother. Some reports suggested she was a prostitute, others said she had died. Either way, it hadn't sat well with his parents. He'd even given interviews about his hatred for his parents and how they had better not show up asking for a handout.

Adam's hands fisted. It was an act. An image created to sway the public into believing good could come from bad. None of it was true. Adam had hated the idea from the start. But that hadn't stopped him from going along with it. All connections to Texas vanished with his new name and look. The country-singer hopeful had become a hard-core rock star.

Adam raked a hand through his freshly shorn hair. The plan had drifted off course. The country labels thought his edgy songs and playing style pushed the genre too much and suggested he either dial it back or head in the hard rock direction. He wouldn't allow anyone to stifle his creativity. Toning it down wasn't an option. Amping it up was.

The money and fame had been amazing at first, but it had come at an enormous expense. His first manager had only seen dollar signs when he'd created Adam's image. But he'd done his job well, because it had gotten Adam in front of the right record labels. When he'd formed his backup band, Adam had kept the facade. Feeling they could do better, the band had collectively fired their manager and hired a new management company. They'd signed a five-album deal within three months. Their big break had arrived and Adam had told his new manager the truth, wanting to end the lies before it cost him more than it already had. But the record label wouldn't budge. They'd bought the entire package and feared they'd lose too much money if Adam's innocuous Texas upbringing was revealed. A booking agent had scored them a world tour and Adam hadn't wanted to risk losing it.

Adam shook his head. There had been ways out of it. He could have easily let it slip in an interview. A random post on any of his social media accounts would have fed the flames enough to get everyone talking. But he hadn't. He'd loved the fame. Loved the money. And he had assumed if he waved enough of it at his family, they'd understand. He couldn't have been more wrong.

He understood why they'd given up on him and why the Katy townsfolk ignored him when he occasionally drifted into town to visit Lizzy. It hadn't been often. A handful of times in ten years. Adam wasn't sure how to win their trust again, but he knew he needed to make some major changes and Ramblewood seemed like a great place to start. Maybe now he could focus on his dream of opening the music school he'd been planning for years.

"There you are." Bridgett leaned over the railing "I should have told you to use the side parking area earlier."

"No biggie." The late afternoon sun cast a soft, warm radiant glow upon Bridgett, almost ethereal. He knew he should stay away from her. Wasn't that what he'd told himself at the restaurant? But he was drawn to her.

Hadn't been able to resist asking her to help him find somewhere to stay. Bridgett intrigued him.

She may be leery of reporters, but she still maintained a cheery attitude toward her customers.

He'd wandered around town for a while waiting for Bridgett's shift to end. He'd met a few people, visited some of the shops and even caught himself smiling in a storefront window. Ramblewood reminded him of home…his real home. He could envision himself rebuilding his life here. Maybe he still had a chance of moving back to Texas.

Adam made a habit of taking each once-in-a-lifetime opportunity that came his way. Sometimes they panned out, but usually they had gotten him into a hell of a lot of trouble. This—Ramblewood—was different and real. For once, Adam vowed to follow his heart instead of doing whatever *his people* told him to do.

"I'm sorry, you'll have to head back to your truck." Bridgett glanced down at her white Keds and sighed.

Adam's heart sank. The disappointment was more than he'd anticipated. "I appreciate you trying, though. I'll check out one of the hotels off the interstate. I do hope to see you again."

"Oh, you'll be seeing me." Bridgett lifted her head and playfully wrinkled her nose as she smiled. "I'll be the one sitting next to you at dinner tonight. Mazie has an incredible meal planned. One of the perks of staying at the Bed & Biscuit. She serves two meals a day."

"I don't understand," Adam said. Bridgett gracefully glided down the stairs. She was still in her waitress uniform but in his mind, she could have been a model on the runway in Milan. He had been invited to quite a few fashion weeks over the years and none of the women compared to Bridgett. Though she had a natural beauty and aura about her—if you plied her with makeup, hair spray and couture gowns, you'd suffocate her. "I can stay?"

Bridgett nodded. "Grab your luggage, and we'll check you in."

Crap. That was something Adam hadn't thought of. Checking in meant showing ID and he no longer resembled his driver's license photo. Plus if he was from Katy, Texas, how would he explain the California driver's license?

After grabbing a small duffel bag from the truck, he met Bridgett inside the inn's foyer. The white-and-red Victorian wasn't the type of place he was accustomed to, but it possessed an inviting charm. And although he'd never admit it to his friends in LA, he'd rather lodge in a quaint and cozy B and B than an obnoxiously garish and overpriced hotel.

"Adam, this is Janie Anderson. She handles all guest relations." Bridgett introduced him to a middle-aged woman coming down a dramatic, richly stained oak staircase ending at a large semi-circle landing that created the room's focal point. "Janie, I would like to introduce you to Adam—I'm sorry, I don't know your last name."

"Steele." He hoped Bridgett hadn't noticed the beads of sweat forming on his forehead. He turned to Janie, "It's a pleasure to meet you."

"She'll register you while I check on your room.

Janie, Adam will be staying in the Balcony Room. I'll
be back down in a minute."

"Oh, you must be one of Mazie's cousins." Janie
removed a leather-bound registry from the front desk
drawer. From the landing, Bridgett shook her head when
Adam almost corrected the woman. Janie ran her fingers across the top edge of the pages until she reached
the ribbon marker, opened the book flat and turned it
to face him. "If you'll fill in your name, address and
phone number—although with you being a relative I'm
sure Mazie has it already—you'll be good to go."

No identification, no license plate number, just a person's word. How ironic that his own family wouldn't
take him at his word, but strangers would. When he
finished filling out the registry, Bridgett was ready for
him. He followed her to the second floor, enjoying the
sight of her bare legs and pert backside while she led
him to his room.

"Here you are. Mazie keeps this room for out-of-
town family, but she made an exception for you. And
before you ask, it's easier for Janie to think you're a
distant relative than endure her third degree." Bridgett
crossed to an elaborate glass-framed and oak-paneled
door. "You have your own private balcony looking onto
Ramblewood Park, a fireplace and a private bathroom.
Mazie decorated this space with mid-1800s Victorian
furnishings. Each room is different, but this is the nic-
est one. Of course, she designed it with pets in mind so
there's no frilly lace to snag tiny toenails. I don't think
you'll find it too feminine."

And feminine it wasn't. Warm, rich oak accents carried throughout the crimson-painted room, from the chair rail to the hand-carved fireplace, giving the space an air of male sophistication.

"It's perfect," Adam said. "How can I repay Mazie for her generosity?"

"Don't break her heart, that's how you can repay me." Adam jumped. A woman in her late twenties stood in the doorway, rivaling Bridgett in height. "I'm Mazie Lawson and welcome to my Bed & Biscuit."

Bridgett gave Mazie a meaningful look. "I apologize for my overly cautious friend."

Adam extended his hand. "It's a pleasure to meet you and thank you for making room for me." Adam wasn't sure what he'd expected Mazie to look like, but he'd figured she would've been more than twenty or thirty years older.

"Well, I need to finish preparing dinner. We're eating at six-thirty. Bridgett, would you mind stopping by Bridle Dance to pick up a sack of pecans Kay has for me? You can take my car. I ran short and I'm determined to win the pie contest this weekend. I won't allow Maggie Dalton to take the blue ribbon fifteen years in a row. And I do wish you'd reconsider not dropping out of the competition. You had your heart set on entering."

Bridgett shook her head. "I'd never beat you or Maggie, anyway," Bridgett said, laughing. "Maggie and Mazie…the two pie queens of Ramblewood. Let me guess. You're going to remain in this house, miss the majority of the festival and bake pies until the contest on Sunday afternoon." Bridgett turned her attention to Adam. "The Magpie was a bakery before it became a luncheonette. Miss Parisian Le Cordon Bleu here is jealous that she hasn't been able to beat a woman who made a career out of pies and cakes."

"*The* Le Cordon Bleu?" Adam asked. "I'm impressed."

"As you should be, *mon cher*," Mazie said in a horribly Americanized French accent before turning to leave. "I must cook. *Au revoir!*"

"I'll head out to the ranch in a bit," she called after Mazie. Bridgett faced Adam. She shifted from one foot to the other and then scanned the room. An awkward silence filled the air as she flicked her thumb under her index finger repeatedly. Adam wondered if she'd just realized they were alone together. "I need to shower away the luncheonette." She inched back toward the hallway. "Would you care to join me—I mean drive out to the ranch with me?"

"Sure, I'd love to see more of your town." Adam's mind veered off in a whole other direction as he envisioned her showering. "Do you live here, too?"

"Temporarily," Bridgett said. "It's a long story. I'll meet you downstairs in thirty."

Adam waited until he heard Bridgett's footsteps fade away before he stuck his head into the hallway. A door closed at the opposite end. Ducking back inside his room, he relaxed against the wall and closed his eyes, amazed how things could change overnight. He had decided to alter his life when he'd left his sister's earlier. A few hours later, a fresh start had fallen into his lap.

BRIDGETT SWORE SHE'D never taken a faster shower. She attempted to blow her hair out, cursing its thickness.

Getting it to a half-way decent point, she reached for her cosmetics bag. The no-makeup look took more of an effort than simply slapping on blush and lipstick.

Almost mid-October and the weather was still on the warm side during the day. The nights brought about a welcoming chill after the scorching summer they'd had. Jeans, a form-fitting tank with a loose white sleeveless linen shirt over it and her favorite inlaid-heart cowboy boots comprised her first-date outfit.

First date? What a delirious thought! A quick run to Bridle Dance for pecans did not constitute a date. An outing maybe. Bridgett slipped her long silver-and-jade pendant necklace around her neck, took one last glance in the mirror and reminded herself to descend the stairs slowly or else she'd end up riding them on her butt. Mazie still hadn't replaced the runner they'd torn out due to a pet guest destroying it a week earlier.

After she said a quick goodbye to Mazie and Janie, Bridgett stepped out onto the front porch.

"Did you even try?" Adam stood near the wrought-iron gate leading to the street, his cell phone to his ear. "Okay, I'm sorry, but you need to understand where I'm coming from, too."

Bridgett knew she shouldn't eavesdrop, but curiosity got the best of her. Not wanting to be seen, she slipped back into the house, listening through the screen. She managed to pick up bits and pieces of the conversation as Adam paced the width of the front yard.

"Lizzy, look at it from my side. This wasn't what I wanted, either."

Lizzy? Could he be married or involved with someone? She hadn't thought to ask. And, why had he been on the interstate driving past Ramblewood? Was he heading to or from home?

Bridgett chewed on the inside of her cheek. How could she be so naive? He could be an ax murderer for all she knew. And here she'd invited him to stay a few feet away from her bedroom. Bridgett covered her face with her hands, debating what to do next.

Take a risk. That's what Abby would do. Her sister had driven all the way to Texas on a hunch, and it had changed her life. Pushing back her shoulders, Bridgett flung open the door just as Adam reached for the handle. Startled, they both laughed.

"Do you want me to drive?"

"Are you married?"

They both spoke at the same time. Adam tilted his head to one side. "Married? No, I'm not married, dating or otherwise attached. You?" Adam asked. "It's not why you're living here, is it? Fight with your husband?"

"No, I haven't been lucky in the love department." Bridgett's toes curled in her boots at the mention of his single status. "The last real date I had was—" Bridgett cut her own sentence short before she embarrassed herself. "Sure, you can drive."

"You look great, by the way," Adam said from behind her. "I like your hair down."

"Thank you." It wasn't the first time she'd ever been complimented, but coming from him it meant more somehow.

THE CAB OF his truck quickly filled with an exotic floral scent when Bridgett climbed in beside him. Adam hoped wherever they headed would take a while. He enjoyed having her to himself, although he'd enjoy it more if his tongue would connect with his brain. Known for usually saying too much, Adam struggled to find ways to keep the conversation going. There was so much about his life he had to hide that it was hard to find a safe topic of conversation. He wondered if Bridgett even listened to his music. Her boots screamed country but he detected a slight edginess waiting to break free. Besides, some of his ballads had actually crossed over to the country stations.

Bridgett directed him where to turn, pointing out various places in town. The freedom associated with driving down rural roads, without traffic, smog and constant noise reminded him of his early twenties, before his world had changed. Wanting to enjoy that freedom, he hadn't turned on the radio since he'd left Lizzy's and unless he was using his cell phone, he kept it off, as well. His voice mail was probably full and he couldn't care less. Adam wanted to remove himself from that world and embrace a simpler life.

"Where were you headed to when you stumbled upon Ramblewood?" Bridgett asked.

"Promise you won't laugh when I tell you." When Adam had decided to drive to California instead of fly, he'd borrowed a pickup he'd purchased for Lizzy but she'd never driven, having said it wasn't her style. "I had planned on taking my dream trip across the United States, visiting all those crazy tourist attractions like the world's largest ball of twine and the biggest iron skillet. I saw it in a movie once, but I never had the time to do it myself. After the falling out I had with my family, I wanted to take a mindless, fun trip." The drive to LA had been a bucket list item he'd decided to knock off while he tried to sort through his plans.

"Falling out?" Bridgett asked. "What happened?"

Adam gripped the steering wheel tighter. He'd said more than he'd intended.

"Let's say I didn't exactly turn out the way my family had expected me to." He wished he could tell her the whole story. But if he wanted a second chance in Texas, he needed people to accept him as he was today. Not as he used to be. Plus, he couldn't take the chance on his transformation and whereabouts being leaked to the media. Not that he thought that was Bridgett's intention, but sometimes people let things slip. No, The Snake needed to stay in the past…for now.

"Understood," Bridgett said. "It's none of my business, really. What was your first stop?"

"I haven't made it there yet. I grew up near the world's largest Igloo cooler. I guess you could say I started my trip with a freebie. My first stop was supposed to be the Toilet Seat Museum in San Antonio followed by the Cadillac Ranch in Amarillo."

"Isn't the Cadillac Ranch the place with the cars sticking halfway into the ground?"

"That's the one," Adam nodded.

"I can understand the cars, but a toilet seat museum?"

"This ninety-something-year-old man has turned a thousand plus toilet seats into works of art over the last fifty years. If he can create it, I can take the time to see it."

"I'm sensing an art theme with you."

"I love art," Adam declared. "Tell you what. If I go to San Antonio, I'll take you with me and you can see it for yourself." Bridgett's face remained stoic. No laugh or smile. Just a continued stare past the windshield. "Was it something I said?"

"No," Bridgett sighed. "Something I promised myself and Mazie earlier."

"I'm a good listener, if you want to talk."

"I promised myself to be free and live more, so yes, I'd love to join you and see toilet seats. But, I promised Mazie I wouldn't rush into anything with you. What she doesn't know—and I'm not sure why I'm telling you this—is that I'm planning to leave town, anyway. As soon as I find a restaurant that I can afford, or one of the places I've applied at hires me I'm out of here. Whether I see toilet seats with you or leave on my own I risk being strangled by my friend. I'm trying to figure out if that's worse than letting myself down by staying put."

Her voice held a twinge of humor, but Adam sensed the weight of the world was on her shoulders as she contemplated her next step in life. But leaving home? He could relate and it didn't sit well with him for some reason. He should stay out of it. It wasn't his place, but he found himself unable to resist trying to reason with her.

"If I may be so bold to offer one piece of advice, and I learned this lesson the hard way: Follow your heart, but don't burn your bridges. It's not always easy to go home again."

Adam turned to see Bridgett watching him closely. A shiver ran up his spine. Suddenly he felt exposed.

"Are things bad with your family?" Her tone was warm, not a hint accusatory.

Unable to speak without his voice cracking, he only nodded. Bridgett reached out and laid her hand on his arm.

"I understand more than you realize," she said softly.

Covering her hand with his, he drove the rest of the way to the ranch in silence.

Chapter Three

Bridgett was a mess. Sitting with Adam's hand over hers, she felt at ease one minute and nervous the next. Who knew one person could hold so much power over her emotions, especially someone she'd just met.

A hint of raw vulnerability had emerged in Adam when he'd owned up to letting his family down. Despite his casual tone, his eyes had betrayed him and held a sense of deep regret. An expression Bridgett knew well—it was identical to the one Ruby wore each time they had crossed paths these past few weeks. Her mother had asked the same of her as Adam wanted from his family. A second chance. Her mother's lies had broken the trust they'd shared. No matter what her mother said, Bridgett had difficulty accepting that she was finally telling the truth. She wanted to forgive her mother, but she hadn't figured out how. So how could she possibly tell Adam not to give up without coming across as an absolute hypocrite?

"Turn left here." Bridgett rubbed the back of her neck, rolling her shoulders. She'd always loved coming out to the Bridle Dance Ranch. Not only had she grown up with the Langtry men, their father had taken time out of his busy schedule to teach Bridgett to ride. And it had been no easy feat thanks to her fear of horses back then. Joe had passed away two years ago, but Bridgett would never forget his kindness and ability to turn a scared little girl into an accomplished rider.

"It's magnificent." Adam peered over the steering wheel and up at the wrought-iron *Bridle Dance* lettering balanced between two rearing bronze horses on either side of the dirt road. "I'd love to know what foundry they used for those horses."

"Foundry?" Bridgett asked.

"The place where they create the mold and cast the bronze."

"Ah, okay." Toilet seats, cars stuck in the dirt and now sculptures…the man definitely had a passion for art…if you could call toilet seats and cars art.

"My sister studied sculpting before she got married."

"She doesn't sculpt anymore?"

"No, her ex-husband almost killed her and brutally broke both her hands. She's never been able to return to it." The words may have flowed freely from Adam's mouth, but his jaw flexed when he spoke, cautioning Bridgett to leave the painful subject alone. "Are those pecan trees?"

Rows of large trees with weeping branches formed a thick canopy above the entrance road, some limbs still heavy with fruit, others almost bare. Men gently shook the branches with a long padded pole as ripe nuts fell to the ground. An older Ford tractor towed a bright red harvester, sweeping the closely shorn grass and gathering the nuts for transport to the pecan cleaner.

"Yes. The Langtrys may use some modern equipment to gather the nuts, but they shake the trees the old-fashioned way. And if anyone wants to pitch in for an hour or two, they're given a ten-pound burlap sack filled with fresh pecans to take home."

"Calling this place a ranch is an understatement." Adam slowly continued past the white-railed fencing that surrounded the pastures and led to the showcase of the quarter-of-a-million-acre property: the three-story log castle—at least that was how Bridgett had referred to it as a kid. The house even had a log turret on the back.

"Pull off to the right and take the driveway to the main house," Bridgett directed.

She hopped from the truck and waited for Adam to join her at the gate leading into the side yard. Reaching over the fence, Bridgett petted Kay Langtry's midnight-black standard poodle.

"This here is Barney." Bridgett squeezed through the gate, grabbed hold of the dog's collar and waited for Adam to enter.

"You don't have to hold him—I'm good with dogs."

"You sure? Because Barney's a wild one."

"Let him go." Adam began to bend forward at the same time Bridgett released Barney. The dog had the upper hand, er, paw, and knocked Adam into the gate.

"Barney, sit!" Kay demanded as she crossed the lawn. "I'm sorry. My boys thought it was cute to teach him to 'give people huggies,' but the dog doesn't know

his own strength. Bridgett, it's wonderful to see you."
Kay gave her a hearty hug. "And who's your young
man?"

"Adam Steele. He's staying at the Bed & Biscuit for
the weekend." Bridgett turned to Adam. "And this is
Kay Langtry, a second mother to most of Ramblewood."

"It's a pleasure, ma'am," Adam said, nodding. "You
have a stunning piece of land."

"Adam was captivated by the entrance sculpture,"
Bridgett said.

"Those were my husband's favorites." Kay laid a
hand above her heart. "If you're not in a hurry, I can
give you a mini tour."

The three of them strolled through the main stables,
or horse mansion as Joe Langtry used to call it, where
Kay introduced Adam to two of her sons, Shane and
Cole. While they talked, Bridgett caught sight of Lexi
exiting one of the stalls. She excused herself and joined
her friend.

"What are you doing here?" Lexi removed her latex
gloves and tossed them into a covered trash bin. "I'd
give you a hug, but I'm horsey and you look stunning
in that outfit. Who's the guy you walked in with?"

"Geesh, you don't miss a thing, do you?"

"Usually not, but I do have to confess. Mazie called
and told me to check out the eye candy you're with."

"Your sister's a real piece of work." Bridgett crossed
her arms. "Did she tell you what she told Adam *before*
I even introduced them?"

"Yes and she told me you looked pretty annoyed

about it, too. He has a sexy rebel vibe going on, doesn't he? What's his story?"

"I'm not sure yet." Bridgett recounted what she knew about Adam, and it wasn't much. "I'm hoping to find out more this weekend."

"How long is he in town for?" Lexi slinked along the stable walls for a better look at Adam, which only made her stand out even more. "Do you need Shane and me to give him a little nudge? We can double-date. My husband owes me a night out."

"Thank you, but—" Bridgett swatted Lexi's arm to stop her from spying.

"Ouch!" Lexi feigned. "What's wrong with you?"

"You're scaring the horses with your prowling. Let's see what happens this weekend before I call in the reinforcements. I have no idea how long he's staying." Or how long she'd remain in town herself.

"This is our Dance of Hope Hippotherapy Facility and the Ride 'em High! Rodeo School." Kay stopped in front of the massive Craftsman-style building. "That's my Joe on top of the one sculpture and my granddaughter on the other."

Adam gazed from the bronzed girl perched on a horse to the twenty-something man atop a bucking bronco. "I take it he was a rodeo man himself."

"Come inside and I'll show you the inspiration photos for both pieces." Kay pushed open the carriage doors leading into a magnificent stone entryway, dividing the two businesses. "This photo was taken during Joe's last ride—my oldest, Cole, was born the next day. And, this one I took the day Joe met my granddaughter, Ever. She was the inspiration for this place."

"Forgive me for asking, but what kind of therapy facility did you say this was?"

Kay beamed at his question. "Come with me and I'll show you."

Adam followed her down a hallway and outside to four separate corrals. Each of them contained a horse, rider and a few other people leading the horse slowly around the grassy area.

"This is hippotherapy." Kay waved to one of the passing riders. "Watch the hind end of that horse and notice how his hips rise and fall. Their walk so closely mimics a human's, by sitting astride a horse, a person with cerebral palsy—like my granddaughter—or a person recovering from a spinal injury, can increase their muscle strength and improve neurological function. It may lead to them walking again. It's not all physical though. We have an occupational and speech therapy side, too."

"I had no idea this existed." Adam rested his arms on the top fence rail and watched the riders. He noted the saddles were different from any saddle he'd seen before. Instead of leather, they were fabric with two large handles on the top for the rider to grip.

Horses' neighs and hooves clomping against the dirt reminded Adam of his parents' ranch. Closing his eyes, it almost felt like home. He opened them as a man in military fatigues rode proudly past. With a few exceptions, most of the patients were children. "You said your granddaughter inspired Dance of Hope?"

"See the rambunctious girl in the far corral." Kay pointed out a tiny brunette with pigtails. "That's Ever. A friend of ours told Joe about hippotherapy and the concept fascinated my husband. By the end of the day, Joe had researched the nearest facility. It was quite a distance from here. He called them up and we took a trip there the next morning. It's where he met Ever. At the time, she was wheelchair-bound. She had grit and determination and Joe loved her the moment they met.

"Ever's adopted?" The girl waved when she spotted her grandmother.

"Since Ever was a foster child, the opportunity for her to continue with this type of therapy wasn't guaranteed. Joe and I had inquired about adopting her, but we were—how'd they put it—above the ideal age range. My son Cole and his wife adopted Ever. Once they'd met her, they had found it impossible to allow her to stay in the system. She's a very special child."

Adam watched the girl dismount next to a platform. "I thought you said she was wheelchair-bound."

"She was." Kay touched Adam's shoulder. "Would you like to meet her?"

"I'd love to."

Despite the greater part of her legs being encased in braces over her jeans, Ever practically ran to her grandmother. Adam found himself battling tears that threatened to choke off his words.

"She can walk because of a horse?" Adam raked his hands down his face. "How come I haven't heard of this before?"

"It's still not widely accepted, but with nonprofits like this one, we're making progress in the field. I only wish my husband had lived long enough to see his dream come true."

"Don't be sad, Grandma." Ever reached for Kay's hand. "Grandpa Joe's watching us from heaven."

Any chance Adam had of keeping his emotions in check would officially be lost if the kid kept this up. Crouching down, he smiled at her. "How old are you to be this wise?"

"Six, but grandma says I'm going on thirty." Ever lifted her eyes to Kay for approval. "Right?"

"Understatement of the year." Kay playfully tugged on Ever's hair. "I'm so proud of you, kiddo."

This was the kind of impact, the kind of good, he wanted to make in the world. Sure, his music entertained people, but it didn't change lives. His money would be much better spent helping others than funding a lifestyle he no longer wanted.

Adam made a mental note to call his accountant later and have a donation sent to Dance of Hope…anonymously.

"I HEARD YOU enjoyed yourself at Bridle Dance," Mazie said to Adam across the expansive dining table.

"Adam hasn't stopped talking since we left." Bridgett playfully nudged him with her knee under the table.

"What's Bridle Dance?" Mrs. Phelps, one of the inn's guests, asked.

"You have to see it," Adam answered before Bridgett had a chance to open her mouth. He leaned forward, his hands moving animatedly as his words tumbled forth. "It's a horse ranch, but they have a center where they use this process called hippotherapy to help people walk again. And a state-of-the-art rodeo school and a pecan grove and—"

"Dearest me." Mrs. Phelps patted Adam's arm. "I'm getting worn out just listening to you."

Adam sheepishly glanced around the table, "Sorry. I guess I'm overly enthusiastic, but amazing doesn't begin to describe it."

"Do you travel much?" Mr. Phelps asked.

"I've been a few places." Adam said.

Bridgett had originally thought a large communal table was an awkward idea when Mazie had first planned the Bed & Biscuit. Who'd want to sit and eat with strangers? She still wasn't used to it, but tonight she loved how the other guests asked Adam questions because she had no clue where to begin without it coming across as an inquisition.

"What brings you in our direction?" Mazie asked. "Katy's not exactly next door."

Adam set his fork on the side of his plate and wiped his mouth with his napkin. "I had a bit of a falling out with my family, and until we can work through it, I thought I'd drive cross-country and take in the sites. I ended up here when I saw the Harvest Festival sign. I had planned only to stay for the weekend, but I might hang around a little longer. If my sister, Lizzy, can smooth things over for me, I'm close enough to get back within a few hours.

"Lizzy's your sister." Bridgett felt her cheeks heat.

"I'm sorry. I accidentally overheard your conversation earlier."

"It's okay," Adam shrugged. "Lizzy's the family mediator and I have no idea which way it will go. Since I'm here, do you think anyone would be willing to hire a stranger?"

Bridgett's pulse increased. Not only did Adam plan to stay past the weekend, but a job meant longer. That meant she'd have the chance to get to know him better. But what if he decided to stay forever? She could be stuck in this Podunk town if she fell for him. On their way home from the ranch, she'd permitted herself the fantasy of leaving Ramblewood with Adam and visiting the ridiculous tourist attractions he had told her about. Crazy? Absolutely. But for a second, it was a possibility. Tucking her head closer to her chest, Bridgett tried to forget the silly notion and focused on her crepes.

Someone bumped her foot and she immediately looked at Mazie, who was passing a dish to Mrs. Phelps. When it happened once more, her eyes met Adam's and his smile told Bridgett he'd caught her thinking about him. Heat rose to her cheeks again. *Oh, please.* She'd rather die than turn into one of those blushing females.

"What kind of work do you do?" Mazie asked, saving Bridgett from further embarrassment.

"My parents own a ranch, and I'm familiar with most aspects of farming and livestock."

"My sister's an equine vet," Mazie said. "I can have her ask around for you."

"Lexi," Adam acknowledged. "I met her and her husband at Bridle Dance."

"They're usually hiring." Bridgett added. She knew Mazie couldn't let Adam remain at the Bed & Biscuit much longer seeing as it was booked for the entire fall season. A job at Bridle Dance meant he'd have a bed in the bunkhouses. "I'll see what I can find out."

"That would be great," Adam enthused. "Thank you."

Bridgett couldn't help feeling excited. It wasn't as if she already had a job waiting for her in another town, after all. She could continue to look while spending time with Adam. It was amazing how much things could change in a day. This morning she'd craved peace and normalcy and by nightfall, she had something much better. Excitement of the sexy male persuasion.

BRIDGETT HAD ALREADY left for work by the time Adam woke the following morning. Braving his voice mail, he switched on his phone. Thirty-six messages and none from his sister. He deleted most of them and called his accountant to arrange for a large anonymous donation to Dance of Hope.

A little before noon, Bridgett knocked on his door. Maggie had demanded she take the rest of the weekend off. Apparently, she hadn't had a day off in almost a month.

"Since I'm free, would you like to go to the festival with me?" Bridgett asked.

"I'd love to."

"Give me a few to change and I'll meet you downstairs."

Adam closed the door and began to gather the notes

he had scattered on the bed. He'd taken a quick trip to the stationery store earlier for some notebooks and pens. He'd had nothing on him when he'd arrived at Lizzy's. He'd left the majority of his personal belongings on the tour bus. It wasn't anything he couldn't replace. And his stage clothes and instruments were in the tractor trailers on their way back to LA.

Adam could use a mental break for the remainder of the afternoon. He'd started a list of people he needed to contact, and had attempted to write his own press release. Well, it resembled one anyway. His publicist would tidy it up. Timing was crucial. But before he did anything, he had to talk to his band.

The way they'd left things that final night hadn't been good. The tabloids speculated this was their last tour. Tours were predictably unpredictable. Shove four grown men inside a tin can for a year, and they were bound to come out fighting. They'd fulfilled their five-album deal and completed a six-continent tour. They had all assumed they wouldn't continue, but nothing was in writing. And until it was, they were still together.

Adam waited for Bridgett outside on the front stairs. The scent of street food and the sound of children's laughter greeted him. Hearing the screen squeak open, Adam rose. Once again, her natural beauty stunned him. She wore a short, pale yellow floral print dress, denim jacket and the same inlaid-heart boots from yesterday. Her hair fell freely around her shoulders and it took every ounce of restraint he had not to walk over and kiss her.

She reminded him of home. Not someone he'd met

before, but the actual comforts of home. Her casualness refreshing. Her smile warm and genuine. Her Texas drawl familiar and inviting. Adam's breath hitched. Was it her? Or was it the idea of her captivating him? If he wanted to be fair to Bridgett, he'd better figure that out before he even thought of kissing her.

"Shall we?" Bridgett stepped onto the walkway and stood mere inches from him. Placing his hand on the small of her back, he opened the gate leading to the sidewalk. He moved them quickly into the crowded streets so he wouldn't be tempted to sweep her into his arms.

What is wrong with me? Adam wasn't the mushy type or even the romantic type. He was the "get in, get out, move on to the next town" type. His schedule was hectic and he only knew two speeds…fast and faster. The entire point of him driving cross country was to prepare himself for a slower, more reasonable pace. Last night he'd told them he wanted a job in town. Not that he needed one, but he wanted one. He craved a life of his own, in a town where people knew him as Adam Steele. It was a fantasy. Once people found out who he really was, that fantasy would end. And whatever was growing between him and Bridgett would likely end, too. His stomach knotted at the thought.

"Candied apple?" Bridgett held a bright red orb on a stick in front of him.

"No, thank you." Adam reached in his pocket and paid for hers before she opened her purse. "I'm more the candy corn type."

"Thank you." Bridgett said, biting through the hard

outer shell, into the juicy apple beneath. "Oh, this is good."

"I bet." Adam swallowed hard.

Good God! It was an apple and she made eating it look seductive. Adam quickly glanced around to see if the rest of the male population was watching, but no one paid any attention to either one of them. It was a surreal experience standing in the middle of a crowd and being able to breathe. No one shouted his name or demanded an autograph. No one pushed or shoved against his bodyguards while he attempted to walk. Yes, he could definitely get used to this.

"We can't miss the parade." Bridgett grabbed his hand, leading him to Shelby Street, where people had begun to line up on either side of the road. "Afterward, we vote on our favorite float and the winner will lead the Christmas parade."

The town erupted in cheers when the parade began. It was impossible not to get carried away with the rest of the crowd. Bridle Dance's float was first—a few of their prized horses pulled a meticulously restored buckboard, with Kay Langtry at the reins. Children filled the wagon with their mothers, waving to the crowd.

"Hi, Adam!" Ever called out to him as she rode by.

Unable to speak, Adam waved in return and wrapped his other arm around Bridgett, pulling her close to him. *Dammit, I want this life.*

They voted for their favorite float and chatted with more people than he'd possibly remember. As they continued to weave through the vendors' tables. Bridgett danced and spun in front of him, modeling a gauzy ivory scarf. Tossing one end in the air, she caught it on the other side of him.

"Now I've got you." Bridgett smiled and tugged him closer. Before he could blink, she released him and turned to pay the man.

"Let me." Adam reached past her, his chest flattening against her back.

"You already paid for my apple." Bridgett tilted her head back, causing their cheeks to rub.

Adam slinked his arm around her waist and twirled her away from the display table. He tucked a folded fifty into the vendor's palm and nodded, silently telling the man to keep the change. When he turned around, Bridgett had draped the scarf around her neck.

"Thank you, again." She smiled. "But no more gifts."

"We'll see." Adam took her hand in his again and they continued to the next table, a local stained-glass artist's.

"I'm really sorry about what happened with Mayor Fox," the woman said while Bridgett peered over the colorful trinkets.

Bridgett froze and Adam swore he heard her teeth grind together. "Thank you." A visible chill passed through her and Adam watched the goose bumps rise on her skin. Turning away, Bridgett shook her head and walked to the next display.

"Bridgett!" A female voice called from behind them. "Bridgett, wait up."

"I think you're being paged?" Adam lightly touched Bridgett's arm to stop her.

"Can't we ignore it, please?" Bridgett reached for his hand and began to walk away.

"Bridgett." A petite blonde ran past them and blocked their path. "I'm glad I found you. Have you thought any more about the wedding?" The woman looked up and smiled at Adam. "Hey, I'm Abby, Bridgett's sister."

"Adam." He shook her hand, trying to read the blank expression on Bridgett's face. "I didn't realize Bridgett had a sister."

"Neither did she up until—"

"Where's your fiancé?" Bridgett interrupted.

Had he heard Abby correctly?

"He's talking to Shane. The Langtrys are going to have a cutting-horse demonstration later at Bridle Dance and an open house tomorrow for Dance of Hope. I'm excited they included me in it since I just started working there. You should come by." Abby turned to Adam. "We haven't met before, have we?"

Adam desperately tried to hide his tension at the question, forcing himself to breathe and relax. Between the haircut, color and sun glasses, he thought he was unrecognizable. "No, ma'am, I'm new to Ramblewood."

"Me, too! I'm still trying to remember everyone's name!" Adam swore if Abby had a set of pom-poms, she'd have done a cheer right in the middle of the street. Adam was so relieved no one had recognized him he'd have joined her in that cheer.

"Here you are." A tall, muscular cowboy approached them and gave Abby a quick kiss. "You're incredibly difficult to find in a crowd. I need to tie one of those old-school bicycle flags on you so I can spot you from a distance."

"Shouldn't you be able to locate me anywhere, Mr. Private Investigator?" Abby rested her head against Clay's chest. "This is Bridgett's friend, Adam. He's new in town, too."

Private investigator? *This isn't good.*

The men shook hands and Adam prayed he wouldn't do anything to raise the man's suspicions.

"I'm Clay. Are you visiting or did you move here?"

"Visiting." Adam noticed Bridgett shift from one foot to the other repeatedly. She was clearly uncomfortable with the conversation and he wasn't feeling too hot with it, either. "Bridgett just finished saying how she wanted to show me something down the street. Would you excuse us?"

Without hesitation, Bridgett chimed in. "I think you'll love it." She linked her arm with his and began to lead him away. "I'll see you guys later."

"At Bridle Dance?" Abby questioned, her brow wrinkled in a plea.

"We'll see how the rest of the day goes," Bridgett said. "I'm not making any promises, but if I can, I will."

Abby seemed somewhat mollified by Bridgett's answer.

"Nice meeting you," Clay said.

"You, too." Adam quickened his pace to match Bridgett's as they moved forward through the masses. Stopping near the corner, Adam drew Bridgett down a side street. "Are you okay?"

Bridgett pushed her sunglasses up, eyes glassy with

tears, and shook her head. "Bear with me. This is hard to explain."

"Come here." Adam protectively wrapped his arm around her and they continued down the street, away from the center of town. Seeing a break between two buildings, Adam tugged Bridgett into the alley with him, away from prying eyes. Resting against the brick facade, he held both of Bridgett's hands in his, waiting for her to speak only when she was ready.

Bridgett suddenly released his hands, slowly lifted his sunglasses and leaned into Adam. Her fingers lightly trailed down either side of his face. "I don't want to talk about it. I don't want to do anything except this." Her lips brushed his, for the briefest of moments, before her body sighed into his and their kiss deepened. Adam knew he should resist. Bridgett deserved to know the truth before giving him any part of herself. But the need to hold her, to feel her in his arms was too strong.

The warmth of her mouth was an invitation while candied apple swirled with her own exotic taste. Adam slid his arms under Bridgett's and he flattened his palms across her spine, drawing her closer. His pulse quickened. Bridgett pressed harder against him and he knew any hope of hiding his desire for her was impossible.

Reluctantly, he broke their kiss, peppering the release with light kisses until they did nothing more than gaze at each other—their breath perfectly synchronized. Neither one of them spoke. Bridgett lifted her fingers to her swollen lips and laughed softly, her eyes wandering down his chest. Her fingertips skimmed over his shirt and Adam was positive she'd feel his pounding heart.

Bridgett shifted closer. Her voice barely a whisper upon his cheek, she said, "I don't want this to end."

Adam wasn't sure if she meant their kiss, or whatever you called the connection developing between them. At this point, it didn't matter. "I don't want it to, either."

Bridgett rolled her head. Stretching her neck, she gazed upward, her body fully touching his again. Adam ran his fingers through her hair, the waves softer than he imagined they would be. He lifted the strands and inhaled her scent before leaving a solitary kiss upon her throat.

"I have to ask you something." Bridgett lowered her head and let out a nervous breath. "How long are you really here for?"

Adam hated to lie. At some point, he'd have to leave, even if it was only temporarily, to finish what he needed to wrap up in LA. He wished he'd met Bridgett on his way back through Texas, not on the way out. He wanted this…he wanted her…but the truth stood between them and he wasn't sure how she'd react when she found out who he was or, more importantly, how he'd hid the truth from her.

He'd felt more alive in the past twenty-four hours and he'd certainly been more truthful than he had in the past decade. He hadn't uttered a single lie. It was what he'd left out that would probably send Bridgett running far away.

"I'm not sure," Adam confessed. "When I pulled into town yesterday, I figured I'd be heading out to-night. Trust me when I tell you, I don't want to leave now that I've met you."

Bridgett laughed and pulled out of his arms. "Ironic, isn't it? I want to leave this place and you want to stay. What if I left with you?"

Her offer was tempting, but Adam recognized a part of himself in her. "You don't have to tell me, but something's obviously wrong." While Adam wanted to reach out for her again, he didn't want to pressure her. "And please don't feel obligated to answer, but what's the deal with you and the corrupt mayor?"

Her eyes widened and Adam wasn't sure if it was fear or shock. "What have you heard?"

"I haven't heard anything. I'm not blind, though. I see how you react when people mention his name."

"I'll give you the abridged version. Abby's my twin sister, but—you're going to love this—neither one of us knew it until a couple of weeks ago. My mother never saw fit to tell me she gave one of us away. Hell, Abby didn't have any idea she'd been adopted—a major shock for her—and the *corrupt* mayor you keep hearing about happens to be our biological father. The secret's out and he suddenly wants a relationship with me. He's seen me practically every day of my life and now he's okay with being my father? Yeah, I don't think so, especially not after I found out he wanted to abort me."

"Bridgett." Adam took her into his arms, uncertain of what to say.

"I need time to wrap my head around this," Bridgett continued against his chest. "I have my mother begging me to forgive her for twenty-eight years of lies and a new sister who decides Clay's the man for her, gets herself engaged, moves to town and is a constant reminder to me and everyone else of what happened. I'm humiliated, hurt and pissed off." Bridgett withdrew enough to look up at him. Swiping at her tears, she continued, "So please forgive me if it's a topic I try to avoid and heaven help the next person who lies to me. I can't deal with one more betrayal."

Adam's stomach turned and his heart squeezed so tightly he thought he might be physically sick. Here he was, another person lying to her. He could tell her the truth, see what happened and be out of her life by morning if she chose. It wasn't fair to build a relationship with her if it meant she'd hate him in the end. He should walk away immediately.

"I need to tell you something." An image of Bridgett slapping him across the face flashed in his brain. Tabloid covers, leaked cell-phone photos, his near arrest in London last month played before him like a music video. "This isn't going to be easy."

"Save it." Bridgett pushed away from him. "I've heard it all before. From *what doesn't kill you makes you stronger* to *your mother meant well*, I've had enough. I don't want to hear it anymore. I'm tired of people pitying me. Hell, I'm tired in general. I want to have fun." Bridgett raised her arms in the air. "Real fun. I want to get out of this place." She grabbed the front of his shirt as she pressed against him again. "Let's go. We'll see all the touristy things you told me about. I can take off alone, but it would be much more incredible if I had someone to share it with. Be that someone. I know you feel the same way. You said it yourself. You had a falling out with your family."

Adam took her face in his hands. "Honey, slow down. Leaving doesn't solve anything. Trust me. I regret it every day."

"Then why are you here?" Bridgett questioned. "If you regret leaving why aren't you back home with your family?"

Adam felt a stab of pain in his chest. He willed himself to breathe. "That's what I'm trying to explain to you. I can't go home. Not yet—"

"Exactly!" Bridgett arched her back. "You do get it. You need time, too."

"No, Bridgett." Adam released her, their eyes locking. "I can't let you run away. Not with me, not like this."

It would be better for her if he just left, Adam knew. He should kiss her goodbye and walk out of her life before he added to her pain. *You don't deserve to kiss her, just walk away.* He'd never managed to make the right choice before, why should today be any different. He tugged Bridgett to him and kissed her, hard and deep.

He broke their kiss and held Bridgett at arm's length. Her chin trembled. She must sense what he was about to do. She began to step away. Her lips pinched tightly to keep from quivering. It was all right. He'd get through it and she'd thank him once the news broke. Bridgett lifted her chin, seeming to steel herself for what came next.

And then he couldn't.

He was too selfish to leave before he even got to know her. So far, she was the one bright spot in his attempt to start over. She might hate him eventually, but maybe she would forgive him. He'd find a way to make things right with his family, and hopefully with Bridgett. It was true… They were in similar situations. They both just needed a little time.

"When do you think you can find out if Bridle Dance is hiring?"

The rigidity flowed from Bridgett's body instantly. He wasn't sure if she was glad he was staying or disappointed they weren't leaving together.

"How about tonight?" she asked.

He nodded. Adam knew it was wrong, but remaining in Ramblewood made sense to him and a job was his best cover until he figured a way out of the mess he had created.

Chapter Four

It was barely Monday when Adam rolled onto his stomach, pulling the pillow down on top of his head. The plaster ceiling hadn't offered much of a view for the past two hours and he needed some semblance of sleep. One problem—his conscience wanted no part of it.

Cole Langtry had asked him to the ranch on Sunday so he could see how well Adam worked the horses. But Adam hadn't expected anyone to hire him on the spot. He had a two-day grace period before starting his new job, and only because they wanted him to start at the beginning of the pay week.

Still stunned the Langtrys had hired him without any form of a background check, Adam knew he was digging himself into a deeper hole with each passing day. What would happen if the truth got out?

It shouldn't matter what the people of Ramblewood thought, but it did. If they were willing to give him a chance, he had to give them a hundred percent of himself. His immediate to-do list had just grown exponentially. He needed to surrender his California driver's license considering he'd told everyone he was from

Katy. It may have been a long time since he'd earned a regular paycheck, but even he knew a driver's license was the first item they'd ask for when he started working. He'd picked up a few bare necessities when he was on the road, but didn't have enough clothes to sustain him very long. And his California cell-phone number was a dead giveaway.

With only two days to reestablish himself as a Texan, Adam prayed they wouldn't ask him to take a driver's test as they had when he'd moved to California. He didn't have much time to get everything done before he raised suspicions as to where he was, and he needed to make sure he did it outside of town. Preferably in San Antonio, where he wouldn't run into someone from Ramblewood.

A faint squeak came from down the hall. If he'd been asleep, he'd have missed it. He rolled, lifting his head and checked the bedside clock. Half past four in the morning. It had to be Bridgett getting ready for work—she'd mentioned she started before five. Who else would be up at this hour?

Dashing into the bathroom, he quickly brushed his teeth. He wanted to charm her, not chase her away with his morning breath.

Easing the door open, Adam peered into the hallway. He tiptoed down the stairs, catching Bridgett before she disappeared into the dining room.

"Adam." Bridgett's hand flew to her chest. "You scared me half to death. You're awfully stealthy this early in the morning."

"I'm sorry. I wanted to wish you a good day." Leaning in, he kissed her softly on the mouth. It wasn't a passionate kiss—he'd keep those on reserve for later. Especially since he heard Mazie bustling about the kitchen a few feet away—people sure were early risers in Ramblewood.

"Are you always this sweet first thing in the morning?" Bridgett tugged at his shirt hem.

"Actually, I've been told by family and friends that I'm a first-class ass when I wake up." Adam wrapped his arms around Bridgett's waist, pulling her closer. "You bring out the best in me."

"Well, I'm glad to hear it, but if we keep this up, I'll be late for work." Bridgett released herself from his arms and stepped back, still holding his hands. "Stop by the luncheonette if you want. I'll be there until two-thirty. Now I must go console Mazie for once again coming in second to Maggie in the pie competition."

Bridgett started for the kitchen, but Adam couldn't resist one more kiss goodbye. It amazed him how clearly he envisioned Bridgett fitting into his life—his new life. He'd easily be able to deal with mornings such as this. Los Angeles was quickly becoming a distant memory. Whether he stayed in Ramblewood or moved back home to Katy, LA was a part of his past.

BRIDGETT HATED HER five-minute walk to The Magpie this morning. She wanted to play hooky with Adam and visit the toilet seat museum. Okay, it wasn't her type of thing, but as much as she'd love to leave Ramblewood for good, she'd settle for a day trip to San Antonio.

She still hadn't figured out what had compelled

Adam to stay. On Saturday she'd had the distinct impression he'd been about to say goodbye. But then he'd asked her about Bridle Dance again.

Apparently Adam had told the Langtrys he wasn't certain how long he'd be in town, but they'd hired him anyway. Regardless of whether Adam stayed or left she knew getting involved too soon would be a mistake. She still had plans to leave Ramblewood and she refused to allow anyone to get in the way. At least she'd have a good portion of the day to keep her mind on something other than Adam Steele.

Bridgett breezed through her morning setup and even found a spare moment to make a peanut pie before the breakfast crowd arrived. Maggie commented on how much more at ease she seemed, which was ironic considering her anxiousness to see Adam again.

The bell jingled atop the luncheonette's doorway, a sound Bridgett would forever equate with the moment she had first laid eyes on him. A tingle traveled the length of her spine. When she turned around, she had hoped to see Adam standing there. The sight of Darren Fox, her biological father, quickly killed her good mood.

"What do you want?" Bridgett spat.

"I thought I told you the other day—you've got no business here." Maggie dashed from behind the counter and stood in front of Bridgett, hands on hips. "I respectfully ask you to leave my restaurant…again."

"Maggie," Darren said. "You can't throw me out."

"Yes, I can, just like your wife kicked your sorry butt to the curb. Think of this as an instant replay. You're officially out. Bridgett told you she needed space and

I told you not to bother her at work, yet you insist on coming in here day after day. Personal issues aside, I won't allow you to harass one of my employees. Don't make me call the law."

"I'm her father."

Bridgett snorted at the declaration.

"Yeah, and it took you almost twenty-eight years to acknowledge her." Maggie turned and steadied Bridgett's hand before she had the chance to hurl the sugar dispenser she'd swiped from the counter. The woman truly did have eyes in the back of her head. "When and if she's ready, it is something to be worked out after business hours. If you keep it up you will find a restraining order slapped across your forehead."

"This is between me and my daughter." Darren remained firmly rooted to the floor. "I spoke to Abby and—"

"Exactly." Bridgett pushed past Maggie. "You spoke to Abby and that's the only reason why you've acknowledged me. If Abby hadn't come to town and your affair with my mother hadn't been exposed, I still wouldn't know you were my mother's sperm donor."

Darren physically recoiled at her choice of words. "A little vulgar, don't you think?" He adjusted his tie as if Bridgett had physically roughed him up, and it suited her just fine, considering she was way past offended at this stage.

"If the sperm fits." Bridgett stormed past Lark, who looked ready to throw knives at the man herself. The other waitress might be new in town, but she'd witnessed almost every encounter Bridgett had had with

Darren. She hadn't hidden her opinions on the situation, either. Something in Lark's past must have triggered her reactions because she'd defended Bridgett as if it were personal.

Running up the back staircase, Bridgett paced the length of the catering kitchen. She couldn't hide out all day, but a few minutes to calm her anger were necessary or else she would break down crying. And she refused to give any of them the satisfaction of seeing her cry. She'd head back down shortly, and if Darren still lurked she'd call the police. She despised the hatred building inside her. It wasn't her nature to stay so angry, but she couldn't seem to work past the feelings.

Tired of the daily drama, Bridgett wasn't sure how much longer she'd be able to control her fury in front of people. By now, half the town would already know she'd almost thrown a sugar shaker at the mayor. It only reconfirmed her desire to escape Ramblewood.

Leaving led her back to Adam. A small part of her wondered if she was only using him as a distraction, and it wasn't fair to either of them. How do you know when your feelings are real? She had the indescribable urge to ask Abby how she'd known her feelings for Clay were true, but Abby wouldn't be able to leave it at that. She'd read too much into it and start grilling her about Adam. It was too much.

In a way, she found herself jealous of Adam. He had the fresh start she desperately wanted. She'd get hers. Until then, she needed to remain focused and patient.

Darren had offered her and Abby money to compensate them for not being around when they were growing up, but both women had refused. Bridgett's shoulders still tensed at the casualness of his offer. As far as she was concerned, Darren had been around the entire time, yet he had actively chosen not to participate in her life. While his money would help her realize her restaurant dream faster, she'd rather work twenty-four hours a day than take one cent from him.

The only problem she foresaw with getting the job that would take her one step closer to that dream was not having a reliable ride to an interview. One of the mechanics from the garage had looked at her car for free last week and told her it wouldn't be much longer before it died. Not what she wanted to hear. He'd promised to look out for a cheap, dependable replacement. Cheap being the operative word. She didn't want to blow any more of her savings than she had to.

Bridgett hated to admit how much she held herself back. She had blamed everyone else, but the truth began to stare her in the face. She had chosen to stay at The Magpie when she could have worked in any of the countless places along restaurant row. Maybe if she had, she'd have more money in savings. And instead of working for someone else, she'd be working for herself by now. But she'd never taken the time to find out.

Bridgett admired Abby's gumption to pick up and move on a whim. She'd chastised her sister for moving because of a man, despite Abby's protest that she'd done it to be near her newfound family. Now Bridgett imagined herself doing the same thing with Adam. Only this time it would be to run from family.

"How are you doing?" Maggie stood in the doorway.

"Is he gone?"

"Yes, and I don't think he'll be back anytime soon."

"I'm sure he'll stop in tomorrow, acting pathetic…if not, it'll be the day after." Bridgett sighed. "He won't go away until I give him what he wants."

"After the way Bert chased him down the street with the soup ladle, I disagree."

Bridgett's laughter echoed throughout the kitchen. "Seriously? I'm sorry I missed it."

"Oh, you would've been proud. Who knew Bert could move that fast." Maggie's face remained serious as a smile began to curl the outer edges of her mouth.

"Thank you, Maggie, for standing up for me." Bridgett hugged the older woman. "I need to do something nice for you and Bert this week."

"You'll do no such thing." Maggie withdrew from her embrace and squeezed Bridgett's shoulders. "My offer still stands if you want to take a week off and get away from here."

"You have no idea how tempted I am. I can't really afford to go solo, though, and my car won't get me very far."

"I'll give you the money, and if you feel you need to repay me, fine. But I wish you'd accept it as a gift. Go somewhere tropical and fun. Fly down to Cancun or Belize and clear your head. They're relatively short flights from here. I think Adam's nice, but I'm not necessarily sure if getting involved with him is the best escape. Don't jump into anything too quickly."

Yet another warning. It wasn't exactly what she wanted to hear, but Bridgett also knew her friends meant well. She loved Maggie, who she knew had her best interests at heart. However, Adam had been the best part of her life recently.

"Maggie, I've already questioned my own intentions." Bridgett tried to find the words to convey how she felt, but if she couldn't describe it to herself how would she describe it to her friend?

"Well, he means something to you. You call it whatever you want." Maggie's brow rose. "Take your time. Breathe."

"I moved out of my mother's house so I could breathe. But I come to work and I still face the daily drama of this whole secret-sister, hidden-paternity nightmare. If it's not Darren, it's somebody else asking personal questions or staring me down. I'm not on display for the world to gawk at. If I leave for a week, it'll just start again when I get back. I'd have to leave town for good."

"You're planning on leaving us?"

"What choice do I have?" Bridgett had wanted to wait until she had a new job lined up before she told Maggie she was leaving. "I'm a constant source of gossip. Abby's a novelty, but I'm the one who's lived a lie in front of everyone. Don't you hear what they say? How they remember me waiting on my father while he pretended I was just another waitress. *Poor Bridgett.* If I hear it once more—" Bridgett balled her fists and paced the room again. "Now his other daughter rolls in and suddenly Darren wants to play daddy. And please, explain why the minute his wife walked out people started to feel sorry for him? He's not a hero for finally doing what he should've done twenty-eight years ago."

Maggie folded her arms and grinned. "There's the

fire I've been waiting for. Get mad, Bridgett. You keep trying to bottle it when it's okay to let it out."

"You don't want me to let it out, Maggie. It won't be a pretty sight."

"I'd rather have you vent on me than leave town. Don't you waste another thought on leaving us. I need to head back downstairs. Lark's working the front alone. Stay up here as long as you want. And remember, I'm always here for you."

"Thanks, but I'm right behind you." Bridgett tightened her ponytail. She should have known Maggie wouldn't take her leaving seriously. "I'm done feeling sorry for myself. If I keep my mind occupied it doesn't hurt as much. Don't worry, I won't go off on another customer."

Maggie linked her arm in Bridgett's. "We'll trade places today. I haven't worked the front in ages. Are you game?"

"You want me to be your pastry chef?" Bridgett had shadowed Maggie when time permitted, but hadn't thought she'd get a chance to work in the kitchen for the entire day.

"It will be good for me to talk to the customers like I used to. I have faith in you. I've seen what you can do. Besides, it will be good training for when you open your own restaurant."

Bridgett longed for that day. She refused to settle for anything less than her dream.

"I've made my decision. I can't take this lifestyle anymore. I'm done." Adam stared out the window of his truck while he waited for the motor-vehicle office to open.

"I hear you." Phil was not only his drummer, they were best friends. "Now that I have a kid of my own, I don't want to tour again."

"Have you talked to Roman yet?" Adam asked. He'd listened to no less than twenty-five voicemail messages from their manager.

"Yeah, basically I told him what we discussed last week, but I left out the finer details. We're through with the gig and pursuing other interests."

"It sounds as if we're launching solo careers."

"I left it open-ended," Phil said. "I don't know where I'm going next. I might do something with a local band or maybe I'll produce. But I can't continue on the way we've been living. I want to be there when my daughter grows up. Not out on the road. I don't want her to learn about her father from the pages of *Rolling Stone* magazine."

While Adam was proud of his Grammy awards and platinum records, he wished he'd done it differently. Too much time had passed. Too many wrongs had gone unnoticed and unforgiven. He'd love to say disbanding the group was his idea, but the reality was they were all ready for a change.

Adam hung up with Phil when the motor-vehicle office opened. Fortunately, the insurance renewal papers on the house and the bank statements on the account Lizzy never touched would prove his residency since they were all in his name. He was glad Lizzy had insisted he take them along instead of her mailing them as she usually did.

An hour later, Adam stared at his temporary driver's

license. He had the surreal feeling he'd time-warped back to his teens. Back in Texas, sitting in a pickup truck, excited about a new job on a ranch and a new girl. He waited for an alarm to go off and wake him from his sleep. None of it felt real. Going unnoticed was as addictive as fame had been.

Arriving back in Ramblewood much later than he had anticipated, Adam slid into the Bed & Biscuit's dining room seconds before Mazie served dinner. Along the way, he'd gained more of a feel for the area and picked up a new cell phone with a Katy, Texas, number. Feeling a bit more secure in his cover, Adam took a deep breath.

"There you are." Bridgett set a stack of plates on the table. "I wanted to call you when I got off work, but I don't have your number. Where did you run off to today?"

Adam told her what he didn't quite think of as a lie, though it wasn't the complete truth, either. "I wanted a better feel for the area so I took a drive and lost track of time. Give me a minute to wash up first and then I'll give you the number."

Adam bounded up the inn's staircase to his bedroom and quickly pulled out his phone to double-check the new number. He had attempted to commit it to memory on the way home but his nerves had betrayed him. It was safer to write it down on a piece of paper and hand it to her.

Adam tried to calm his nerves with a few inhalation breathing exercises he used to run through before a show. Bridgett made him more nervous than playing onstage in front of eighty-thousand screaming fans. Still unable to pinpoint the hold she had over him, Adam decided to go with the feeling and enjoy the moment. The sooner he did damage control, the sooner he could tell Bridgett the truth.

He found her waiting for him at the bottom of the stairs. She stood to face him, a slow smile forming as be approached.

"How about grabbing a bite to eat elsewhere tonight?" Bridgett asked.

"Are you sure Mazie's okay with us leaving? I thought you were kind of obligated to eat here."

"Not at all." Bridgett took his hand in hers and led him outside. "I let Mazie know earlier we might go out tonight, but she prepared extra in case we changed our minds. I wasn't sure what you wanted to do, but it's too gorgeous to stay inside. I love the fall."

"Lead the way."

The sun had already begun its final descent for the evening, casting shades of red and gold against the western sky. Before they reached the porch stairs, Bridgett put her arms around his neck and kissed him with a fire he could only compare to that of a military wife seeing her soldier for the first time in ages. He'd witnessed a handful of those surprise reunions during his last USO tour.

Adam had had many women kiss him, but none as passionately as Bridgett. He hated how he'd just compared her to other women. When she found out the truth, she'd inevitably ask if he compared her to any of them. They always did. When you'd been around so many groupies, a certain lifestyle was assumed. She wouldn't be far off with her assumptions in the female-companion department. It was a conversation he dreaded having with her if they ever reached that stage.

Bridgett's brazenness bothered Adam a bit. It wasn't the kiss, it was how she kissed him on the front stairs of the Bed & Biscuit—near the center of town—for everyone to see. Adam felt more like a prized bull on display for people to admire than—than possible boyfriend material. Whatever they were, Adam's gut instinct told him Bridgett wasn't a wild child. While he'd gladly accept any kiss from Bridgett, a staged one wasn't on the list. The stiffness in her body only confirmed his suspicions.

Setting her away from him, Adam stared into her piercing green eyes and tried to make sense of the situation.

"What's this really about?" He pushed a stray lock of hair out of her face. "You're different tonight."

"Who says it has to be about anything except me wanting to be with you?" Bridgett took a step forward. "Tell me you didn't miss me today and I'll back off."

"I can't," Adam admitted. "I'd be lying"

Seemingly satisfied, Bridgett strode down the walkway. Unlatching the iron gate, she held it open for him to pass through. "I'm not sure how to take you."

Adam followed Bridgett onto the sidewalk and twirled her into his arms. "Why don't we take it day by day and see where it goes? But I have to ask… When you kissed me on the porch just now, was it because you really wanted to kiss me or was a part of you saying to the town, *'Hey, I'll give you something to talk about'*?"

Bridgett flinched at his question and Adam immediately regretted asking it. "Forget I asked."

"No. You're partially right, but not for the reasons you might think. I am so sick and tired of everyone's pity I wanted to show them I can be happy and I can move on. It wasn't to show you off or try to take center stage. I'm in the spotlight as it is and I'd like the curtain to fall."

He, more than anyone, could understand that. Drawing her into his arms, Adam gently kissed Bridgett until her body softened against his. He had a sneaking suspicion if he opened his eyes, he'd catch everyone in the Bed & Biscuit peeking through the window at them, but none of it mattered. He wanted to relish the kiss. He'd taken too much for granted and wanted to savor his time with Bridgett.

Reluctantly he released her, and they continued walking toward the center of town. "Where would you like to eat tonight?"

"If you like Mexican, we can go to The Whole Enchilada on restaurant row." Bridgett pointed ahead. "It's only a few blocks down, along Cooter Creek."

"Mexican it is." Adam wanted to slow their pace tonight. Once they returned to the Bed & Biscuit, he would have to start mentally preparing himself for the conversations he needed to have tomorrow. Namely with his manager and sister. The sooner they both knew he had officially severed ties with the band, the sooner his new life could begin. It was the first step in winning his parents' trust. Adam hadn't wanted to break Bridgett's trust in the process, but it was inevitable. Hopefully she would understand why he'd had to keep the truth from her.

"HAVE YOU SPOKEN any more with Abby?" Adam asked as they finished their enchiladas.

"No, and now that you mention it, she didn't stop by The Magpie." Bridgett would've accepted an entire day with Abby in exchange for one minute with her biological father. "Instead Darren paid me visit."

"How did it go?" Adam's concerned expression warmed Bridgett.

"I told him off and Bert chased him down the street with a ladle."

"You're kidding me?" Adam covered his mouth with a napkin. "Remind me to thank this Bert character. He definitely sounds like he's a member of your fan club."

Bridgett watched Adam's expression go from jovial to almost painful in under a second.

Adam reached across the table for Bridgett's hands, pulling her attention back to him. "Do you think you'll ever want a relationship with your father? And no, I'm not judging. I'm in no place to do so."

"I don't know what I want yet, which has been the problem. This happened so unexpectedly. When Abby left to confront her parents, I thought I'd have a break from the situation. I wasn't expecting Clay to follow her and drive back with a U-Haul truck filled with all her belongings. It's not that I have anything against Abby. I guess a part of me is jealous. She has a nice car, an amazing career…and Darren was more interested in her life than he was in mine."

"I don't understand how he could ignore you all these years. You never noticed anything strange between him and your mom?" Adam turned her palms upward and stroked his thumbs across them.

Bridgett shook her head. "Not at all. It's a small town, they ran into each other a lot, but I never sensed anything inappropriate between them. They didn't try to avoid each other, either. They didn't exactly run in the same social circles though. But would you believe she cut his hair all this time? It didn't seem like an unusual relationship until Abby came to town. Then things got weird. Mom became scatterbrained and weepy all the time."

"Did she realize Abby was her daughter?"

"She claims she didn't at first, but after talking to Abby a few times she figured it out. Abby had been vocal in her search for me, but little did Abby know she was looking for her long-lost mother, too." Bridgett shuddered at the memory of the night her mother had told her and Abby they were sisters. The confusion still hadn't lifted.

"I'm sorry. I don't mean to pry." Adam released her hands and reclined against the back of the chair. "I have my own mess to straighten out and I shouldn't be digging into your personal life."

"I'm available if you want to talk about it. What do they say…the best lovers are friends first?" Bridgett's own statement surprised her and she silently applauded her inner seductress.

"Don't tease." Adam winked. "Now I won't be able to get that image out of my head tonight. You better be careful, Little Miss Ramblewood."

"Why?" Bridgett sucked on the lime slice from her drink. She was teasing and she enjoyed it. It came naturally with Adam. After countless failed blind dates where Bridgett had fended off advances, it felt good being the one to make the first move.

"I might take you up on your offer." Adam slid his chair closer to hers. "You were offering, right?"

Bridgett threw her head back and laughed. "Wow! If you can't tell I'm flirting with you then I'm extremely rusty at this." She lifted her hand and lightly ran her fingers along his jaw line. "Thank you for making me laugh. I haven't done much of it lately."

"You don't need to thank me. Just promise me you'll continue to be happy." Adam's mouth was inches from her ear. "And don't be in such a hurry to leave town."

Bridgett straightened. "Why? You're not planning to stay in Ramblewood forever. The day will come where you reconcile with your family and leave our little burg. Why should I stay for you when you don't plan on staying for me?" Bridgett couldn't stop herself. The words slipped out of her mouth before she'd been able to stop them.

"Which one is it?" Adam's brow creased. "One minute you want to leave town, the next you seem upset that I might leave. For the record, if things work out with my family—I don't necessarily think I'd move back there. Three hours isn't far from here. Besides, even when I lived in Katy, I didn't see them every day. My goal is to repair the relationship, not move in with them. There's no reason why I can't continue to live here…unless you don't want me to."

"Not at all. I don't mean to imply otherwise. Well, that's not entirely true." Bridgett inhaled deeply. "I want out of Ramblewood. I have hopes and dreams and I can't picture them happening here anymore. I'm afraid that if you stay in Ramblewood it will be even harder for me to leave. But I don't want to ruin your happiness, if you think you've found it here. Do you really believe you'll be happy in this little town, working as a ranch hand? When you got here you were excited to see all those places from that movie—toilet seats, buried cars… But you must have bigger dreams than that. Don't you?"

Adam hesitated, and Bridgett eagerly awaited a deeper glimpse into the man next to her. "I'd like to keep spending time with you, get to know you better. But I want to stick around Ramblewood for a little while. There's been so much fighting in my family, so much chaos in my life lately. I just need to take some time out and direct my attention elsewhere. A ranch job is very cathartic—hard, physical work keeps me from dwelling on my problems. That doesn't mean I'll stay in Ramblewood forever, but for the moment I'm happy to be here."

Bridgett forced a smile, but inside her heart was sinking. She'd thought maybe Adam could be part of her new beginning, but he was more likely to keep her trapped in Ramblewood if she let him. Plus, he still hadn't told her what he wanted out of life. He also hadn't given her any details about his battle with his family.

She wanted to get to know him better, but it felt as if there was a wall she couldn't see past.

Tension buzzed between them instead of the electrifying sparks they'd experienced on their walk to the restaurant. "Maggie let me work in the kitchen as pastry chef today instead of waitressing," Bridgett said. Maybe the subject change would recapture their earlier energy. "I've been her catering assistant for the past few years, but I've only had the opportunity to experiment when The Magpie was slow. Today was amazing. It was the first time in a long while that I was able to spend some decent time in the kitchen. I can't wait to open a restaurant where I can create my own recipes and menus. Hopefully I won't have to be a waitress much longer."

"Nothing wrong with waitressing." Adam gave Bridgett's hand a reassuring squeeze, one that annoyed her more than comforted. "You live a simple life here in Ramblewood and I'll be the first to admit I'm jealous of it."

He must be kidding! Bridgett held her tongue as the waiter set a dessert plate of churros between them. "There's simple and then there's boring." She was stuffed from her chicken enchilada but the scent of cinnamon sugar and fried dough became impossible to resist. She broke off a piece of churro and popped it in her mouth. "Oh my stars, this is good."

She wiped at her fingers then glanced up at his handsome face. If only she could make him understand. "The Magpie's the only job I've ever had. I've learned a lot about catering and restaurant management from Maggie, and Mazie's taught me some of the finer techniques she learned in Paris. She's also gone into more depth on small business finances. I've always pictured myself running my own place—American food, small and quaint... Wow, I really am boring. My vision doesn't stray very far from my reality." She sighed inwardly. "I guess I might as well just stay in Ramblewood and buy The Magpie from Maggie one day."

Adam bit into a piece of churro, sugar speckling the fiesta-stripe tablecloth. "You're far from boring. Don't put yourself down. Expanding on what you already know is how people get ahead in business."

"I'm in dire need of new experiences. I've never been anywhere." Bridgett shrugged. "I've certainly never been as far east as Katy. Well, I did go to Vegas but we flew, so I didn't get to see much of the country. I'd love to travel the world and really see what's out there. I want to experience life instead of just living it."

Adam reached across the table and wiped a dusting of sugar from Bridgett's chin. The gentleness of his touch sent a flush of heat through her body. "Maybe you haven't done those things because it wasn't your time yet."

She used to believe things happened for some greater purpose, but now those beliefs seemed naive. If she wanted her life to change she'd have to take action. "I may never be able to afford to travel all the places I want to see, but I'll certainly try. I don't have a destination in mind, although your cross-country trip does have some appeal. I wouldn't mind seeing the biggest ball of twine."

Adam flagged their waiter for the check. When it arrived he released her hand, removed a couple of twenties from his wallet and slipped it into the restaurant billfold. "Well, maybe you'll stay long enough for us to take that trip together."

"Maybe." Bridgett removed a hand-sanitizer sachet from her bag to wipe away the remainder of the sticky sugar residue from her fingers. "I wish I knew what drew you to this town, though."

From the other side of the room, a woman shrieked. They both looked in her direction as a man knelt down on one knee and held a ring box open in front of his girlfriend.

"Yes!" The woman shrieked again. "Of course I'll marry you."

Bridgett turned to Adam and found him studying her. "I'm looking at the answer."

"Excuse me?"

"You asked what drew me to Ramblewood." Adam cupped her chin. "I'm looking at her."

Chapter Five

Back at the Bed & Biscuit, Adam walked Bridgett to her door. It was almost midnight and the inn was silent except for their whispers in the hallway. Adam hated to say good-night, but it was too soon to ask Bridgett to stay with him. He kissed her softly, loving the feel of her lips beneath his, her body pressed against him. Then she slipped out of his arms and sagged against the doorjamb.

"How do I know this is real?" Bridgett's pupils dilated in the dim light. "You had a whole other set of plans before you arrived here. And I sense there's something more, something you're not telling me. I've been through enough of my own crap to recognize that you're in the middle of something major."

A floorboard creaked across the hall, shattering their attention. They needed somewhere private to talk, because what he needed to tell her required a lot of explanation.

"What's below my room—the sitting area?" Adam kept his voice barely above a whisper.

"Yes, why?" Bridgett asked.

"Come to my room," Adam said, lightly tugging her to him. "To talk, nothing more."

For a moment, Adam thought Bridgett would follow. His palms immediately began to sweat in anticipation of her reaction to the truth. She hesitated again, and lowered her eyes to the floor.

"Not tonight." Her voice was timid, almost shaky. "We both know it won't end with talking. I'm not sure we're there just yet—not because I don't want to. I do, and I realize I've been sending you mixed signals, but I need to be sure. I don't think I can face any more heartache."

"Shh, I understand. I'm in no hurry." Adam kissed Bridgett again and watched her disappear behind her door. Twice he'd tried to tell her the truth and failed miserably.

In his own room, Adam paced the floor. Why was the truth so difficult to admit? He knew the longer he kept it from her the more betrayed she'd feel. He didn't want to hurt her, but he didn't want to lose her, either. He needed to come clean before he wounded her beyond repair.

It may have been late in Ramblewood, but by Los Angeles standards, it was still early. Pulling his old cell phone out of his bag, he turned it on and ignored the voice-mail messages. He needed to call his manager before he lost his nerve.

Roman hadn't been completely blindsided by the news thanks to Phil softening the blow. The rumblings amongst the band members that this would be their last tour had grown louder in recent months, as well. Roman had probably seen it coming.

"I'd rather see you end things now than have the four of you destroy yourselves. Plus, there's always the possibility of a reunion tour a few years from now. Fans will pay good money for that."

"That's pretty much how we saw it, too. I spoke with Phil earlier today and he told me he plans to focus on his family. I can't blame the man. We all need a break."

"You especially," Roman agreed. "I'd like to go a solid year without seeing your name in the news. I'm fine with you taking a break and everyone figuring out what they want to do next. I hope you realize you're not just a paycheck to me. We've all become friends through this crazy ride and I'm always here if you need me."

Adam had grown to think of Roman as family. He couldn't count the number of holidays and birthdays they'd spent together. "I appreciate it. As far as announcing this publicly, I'm torn over the best way to handle it. I'd like a little time before you do because I need to prepare things on my end. I think my remaining corporate sponsors should know ahead of time. I'm assuming they'll want to prepare their own statements. My family will probably be mobbed by tabloid reporters camping out on their doorstep." Adam rubbed his temples. He hadn't considered that possibility before. It was the last thing he wanted or they needed. It certainly wouldn't help his relationship with them any. He tugged a notebook out of his duffel bag and added to his to-do list, which had tripled in length over the last twenty-four hours. He'd have to put security in place to help shield his family from the fallout. "We need a collective statement from the band along with a personal one from me. I've already prepared mine. I don't even know if JP and Dave want to be in the country when the news breaks. Phil already told me he's planning to stay with his wife's family in Ireland for a few weeks."

"Absolutely. Send me what you have and I'll have a talk with your publicists. There isn't much to do on this end." Roman's reassurance helped calm Adam's nerves. "We've fulfilled all your contractual obligations and we'll stop the promoters from booking any further dates. I hate to say it, Snake, but after the way this last tour ended my phone isn't exactly ringing with offers. To be honest, if you hadn't decided to do this, I probably would have told you to anyway. Clear your head."

Adam eased into the wingback chair near the window. As much as he wanted this to be over with, he knew the timing was crucial.

"Thank you. I need to right quite a few wrongs, but I'm afraid I'll hurt many people in the process. I've already destroyed my relationship with my family and their faith in me. They were the ones who nurtured my desire to be a musician in the first place." Adam had rejected every value his parents had instilled in him and it sickened him to know he'd allowed it to go on this long. "And when I attempt to correct that damage by telling everyone where I really came from, I'll lose the respect of my fans. Once they learn I've lied to them, they'll want nothing more to do with the band or me. I'm not only obliterating my own reputation, I'm effectively killing Phil's, Dave's and JP's, too." The ripple effect had the potential of reaching far beyond the band. Adam couldn't even remember how many fan letters he'd received from battered and broken kids who looked to him as their role model. If he could survive and make it off the streets, so could they. But he was a fraud. "The only reason why I lived with the lies so long was because I was greedy. It didn't matter what the label said. It was my life and I should have stood up to them. The money wasn't worth what it cost me in the end."

Adam was ashamed to speak the words. For far too long he'd passed the blame on to everyone else. It was all him.

"I know I've told you before how I wished I'd represented you in the beginning, but you have to admit— The Snake was a global success. It's hard to turn back the clock. It's time to focus on the future now. What's next for Adam Steele?"

"I want to open the music school I've told you about over the years." Adam wished he could have told Bridgett about his ideas earlier in the evening. After years of planning, Adam finally had a chance to see those plans through. Not only would people of all ages be able to take lessons on every instrument imaginable, but he wanted to have a recording studio within the school, as well. His students would have the ability to record and learn all aspects of the industry from song writing to sound engineering and mastery. Telling Bridgett would lead to questions about his background and the more she asked or told others, the bigger the risk they'd discover who he was. He had to keep it to himself for a little while longer.

"I hope it works for you," Roman said.

Adam stood and walked back to the bed where he'd left his notebook. He flipped it open and removed a wrinkled sheet of paper with a sketch of the floor plan. "Once the news breaks people will know my real name. Either it will help me get students or I'll have none. Regardless of the lies, I'm a damn good songwriter and musician. My musicality doesn't fade with the lies. I hope people realize that, but I'm prepared for the worst."

"Do you want it worked into the press release?"

"No." Adam shook his head knowing Roman couldn't see him. "It makes me sound less sincere if I'm hyping a new business in the middle of apologizing for duping the world." Adam refolded his school plans and added another line to his list. "I do want to issue a personal apology to the crew though. I hate letting them down along with everyone we've worked with on tour. But it's time. I need to put The Snake behind me and live my life as Adam Steele again. I'm enjoying the anonymity. I won't give you all the details because I need to keep this to myself for now, but trust me when I say it feels good."

"What do you need me to take care of for you?" Roman asked.

"I'm going to need my house discreetly packed up and I don't know who to call. I want to put it on the market immediately, but once I do, it will create a media nightmare. The vultures will start spinning stories the instant they see a moving van pull through my gates. That's one of the reasons why I'm hesitant to do it today."

"Your neighbors will probably throw you a huge going-away bash. Maybe you should wait a bit."

Adam winced. "I don't think I understood how many people I'd pushed too far until this past week. I kept convincing myself as long as I created music, and people bought and enjoyed it, then who cared what I did." He'd fooled himself into thinking he created more joy than misery.

"It's been years since I've heard you this levelheaded. You lost that spark of excitement for what's next a long time ago. However you've found it again, I'm just glad you did."

Adam finished his conversation with Roman and sat outside on the balcony for a long time afterward contemplating what his manager had said. Roman was right. He had lost interest in everything, going through the motions of the day. He'd done what his handlers told him to do, not thinking much on his own along the way. When thoughts did start to fill his head, he'd throw a party or spend exorbitant amounts of money on the most frivolous crap...because he could.

Adam cringed at how horrible he had become. He wanted to make up for it now, if he could. And the first place to start was with the wonderful woman down the hall.

THE FOLLOWING MORNING, Bridgett paused outside Adam's door before she headed downstairs. She listened, but didn't hear a peep from inside his room. Slightly disappointed, she knew she couldn't expect Adam to greet her this early every day. Considering he'd be moving to the

Bridle Dance Ranch soon, she supposed she shouldn't get used to seeing him in the morning.

Sighing, she turned to walk toward the stairwell, but Adam's door swung open and he pulled her inside.

Pressing her against the wall, he brought his mouth down firmly on hers. "You didn't think I'd let you leave without a kiss, did you?" Adam whispered against her lips.

"I wasn't sure if you were awake."

"Exactly what I wanted you to think." Adam grinned. "I knew the minute your feet hit the floor."

"What did you do, camp outside my room for the night?" Bridgett asked.

"Did you know there's a loose board in your room? It's not loud, but sound definitely travels in this place when everyone's asleep."

"I'll have to mention that to Mazie. We wouldn't want her guests being disturbed in the middle of the night."

Adam slanted his mouth over hers again, his kiss warm and inviting.

"I—um—better head to work." Bridgett forced herself to slide from his embrace. "I'll see you later."

Still in a daze from Adam's kiss, Bridgett almost slipped down the stairs. Gripping the railing tighter, she inwardly laughed at herself. A broken leg was the last thing she needed on her birthday.

"Are you okay?" Mazie peered around the corner.

"I'm fine. When are you getting a new runner anyway? You're lucky it was me and not a guest." Bridgett inhaled the aroma of fresh coffee and chocolate chip pancakes.

"They're coming to install it this afternoon." Mazie steered Bridgett to the kitchen's bistro table where a stack of pancakes awaited her. "Happy Birthday! I'm not making these for the rest of the house. This is special for you only."

"Thank you." Bridgett poured warm maple syrup over her breakfast. "You didn't have to do this, but I definitely appreciate it." Bridgett lifted the fork to her mouth. "Mmm. Much better than that pancake chain in Kerrville."

"That's quite a compliment." Mazie joined Bridgett at the table with her own plate. "Do you have any other plans for today besides work?"

"None." Bridgett sipped her coffee. "Mom texted yesterday and asked me to a joint party for Abby and me at Slater's tonight, but I'd rather not. I have to give her credit for texting rather than calling or coming to see me. She's kept her distance like I asked."

"Isn't there something you want to do after work rather than come back here?" Mazie asked. "I'm surprised Adam doesn't have the afternoon planned?"

Bridgett shook her head. "Adam has no idea it's my birthday."

"What?" Mazie almost dropped her fork. "Why not?"

"Because I don't want him to fuss over me. And don't you tell him, either." Bridgett waved her fork at Mazie. "It's better this way. Besides, he bought me a scarf on Saturday and that's gift enough for me."

"I think you should tell him, but far be it from me to get involved."

"Oh, sure." Bridgett rolled her eyes. "Far be it from you to ever get involved in someone else's life. Definitely not your style."

"What are you implying?" Mazie straightened and frowned at her.

"Nothing." Bridgett knew Mazie wanted the best for her friends and family, taking on a role way beyond her years. She may be Lexi's younger sister, yet she acted more like her mother than their own mother did. "I wouldn't have you any other way."

"Hold up a minute, stud." Mazie called from the kitchen. "I need to talk to you."

Adam slowly turned to face her, uncertain what to expect. "Good morning."

"Good morning. Listen, today's Bridgett's birthday and I am putting together a little celebration dinner for her here tonight."

"I had no idea. She never said a word." Adam chastised himself for not asking Bridgett when her birthday was after she had mentioned it was coming up the other day. "Are you asking me to join or stay away?"

"Why would I ask you to stay away?" Mazie tilted her head.

"I get the impression you don't exactly like me," Adam replied.

"I have nothing against you." Mazie poured Adam a cup of coffee and handed it to him. "I don't want to see Bridgett hurt any more than she already has been, that's all. Of course, you are invited. Lexi and Shane will be joining us, too. I've already arranged for my inn guests to enjoy dinner on me at one of the local restaurants, leaving the night clear for us to celebrate her birthday without me having to worry about this place."

Adam wasn't sure how Bridgett would feel about a birthday party this year because of all the lies she'd been told about her birth. "Bridgett's mom and sister aren't coming?"

"I didn't invite them." Mazie shrugged. "There's a celebration planned at Slater's Mill later for the two of them but Bridgett has no intention of going, so I think she'd rather steer clear of her family tonight. I don't know how she will react to the party, but I figured if she wanted to celebrate with anyone, it would be you."

Adam smiled at the unexpected compliment. He hadn't been certain how much he'd come to mean to Bridgett until Mazie confirmed it. "I have no idea what to give her." Bridgett had seemed uncomfortable when he'd paid for her scarf and candied apple at the Harvest Festival. "Any suggestions?"

"Bridgett doesn't own much," Mazie said. "She moved in here with a couple of suitcases. Those cowboy boots she wears all the time are the one pair she owns. Outside of her work sneakers, she has maybe two pairs of heels. She doesn't even own a computer. She either uses mine or heads to the library. She has her car and it's amazing it hasn't fallen apart in the parking lot already. Bottom line, she isn't very materialistic so there's nothing you can buy her that she would appreciate more than just having you around."

Adam hadn't taken the time to think about what Bridgett did or didn't have. He knew she had moved into the Bed & Biscuit after leaving her mother's house, but the prospect of her owning nothing else hadn't crossed his mind. All the women he knew in Los Angeles acquired more junk than they had room for...especially when it came to clothes and shoes.

"She does have pierced ears though." Adam remembered seeing a jewelry store on Main Street.

Mazie nodded. "I don't think she wants you to buy her a gift, Adam. Between the situation with her mother and just meeting you, it might make her feel awkward. But I can already see you're not going to listen to me, so if you do buy her something don't spend too much. She's not that type of girl."

"Thank you for the advice." Adam tried to think of something related to cooking, but he hadn't seen any kitchen stores in town. Not that Bridgett had a kitchen of her own. "Can I help you with anything this morning?"

"No, but thank you for asking." The hint of a smile told Adam that Mazie was beginning to warm up to him. "I'm sure you have your own plans before starting your new job tomorrow."

"A few." Adam had to fill Lizzy in on what to expect when the truth came out. She was his only way of reaching his parents and the more he thought about it, the more he was convinced it would be better for them to be far from home when the news broke. But his father would never abandon his ranch, not even with a full security detail on the grounds. "What time's the party tonight?"

"Lexi and Shane will be here around six." Mazie checked her watch. "I'll need you to keep her occupied elsewhere this afternoon so I can set up—I want tonight to be a surprise. I don't want her to come here after her shift at The Magpie and start cleaning this place. That's out of the question on her birthday. But Bridgett's stubborn. It will take some doing on your part to keep her away."

"Sure. What won't make her suspicious though?"

"Take her pumpkin picking."

"Take her what?" Adam laughed.

Mazie ducked into the kitchen and returned with her purse. "Tell her I asked you to get them today because by the weekend the patch will be picked over. I always decorate the front of the inn with pumpkins, and if time permits I'll hand-paint some of them. Bridgett will know what sizes I need. It should keep you two occupied for a few hours." Mazie removed some bills from her wallet and handed them to him. "This should cover it. And don't let anyone talk you out of paying for them, either. I need too many pumpkins to keep getting them for free. It makes me feel guilty."

"Then pumpkin picking it is." Adam couldn't remember the last pumpkin he'd picked or carved. It must have been with his mother and sister when they were kids. Dad would have been too busy to join them. One year they grew their own. They hadn't gotten very large, but it had been fun for two little kids to turn the pumpkins every day so they wouldn't rot. "Do they have any corn field mazes nearby?"

"My family's farm, that's where you'll get the pumpkins, has one the night before Halloween. It's enough to scare the bejesus out of you. It's open for one night only and my brother's in charge of it. The way he has it rigged, I guarantee it will take ten years off your life. I won't go through it anymore."

"I hadn't realized you were raised on a farm." For some odd reason Adam had difficulty envisioning Mazie working in the fields. She seemed more of a city-bred girl.

"Born and raised. My entire family—aunts, uncles, cousins—all live out there. We have a petting zoo, a country store complete with a country kitchen. Lawson's Farm is the local tourist attraction for people coming off the interstate. You would have passed it on the way in. I guess it was only fitting I opened up a bed-and-breakfast."

Adam regarded Mazie. She and Lexi couldn't have been more different. While Lexi was a tall thin brunette who looked as if she was completely at home working in a barn, Mazie's softer silhouette and reddish-blond hair enhanced her more sophisticated appearance. He couldn't picture Mazie digging in the dirt, but definitely could envision her at the helm of a five-star restaurant.

"I know my staying here was unexpected and probably against your better judgment," Adam said. "I wanted to thank you. I appreciate you renting me the room you reserve for your family. I'll be out of your hair by the end of the week once I settle in at Bridle Dance."

"You're welcome. I will admit I was uncertain about your relationship with Bridgett. I'm less so now. You seem to be a fairly decent guy and as long as you don't break her heart, I think we'll get along fine."

If that hadn't made Adam feel guiltier than a puppy standing next to a puddle, he didn't know what would. "I understand why you're protective of her."

"I think Ruby meant well by keeping her secret about Abby and Bridgett. But the way she dealt with it afterward left a lot to be desired. Ruby did an awful lot of fawning and bragging that her newfound daughter is a physical therapist. She rambled on and on about Abby's accomplishments to anyone who'd listen. You could see Bridgett shut down when Ruby carried on. Bridgett won't say anything because she doesn't want to appear petty or jealous. But between Darren's three kids and Abby, Bridgett feels left behind when it comes to education."

"What does she want?" Adam asked. "Apart from opening a restaurant. Is there anything else?"

"Somewhere she can call her own. Bridgett can stay here as long as she pleases, but for her own sake, I hope she gets an apartment. It would give her a sense of accomplishment. Has she told you she's looking for a job outside of town?"

Adam stared at Mazie. Bridgett had said no one else knew of her plans and Adam wondered if Mazie had set a trap for him to divulge her secret. "Plans?"

"Bridgett forgot to clear the browser's history the other day. I saw every job she'd applied for online." Mazie sighed. "She has told you, hasn't she?"

"Yes." Adam hesitated, measuring how much he should say. "If it's any consolation, she hasn't heard back from any of them. I've tried to talk her out of leaving, but she's determined to do it."

Mazie clasped her hands over Adam's. "Please continue to try. And don't forget about tonight."

"Leave it to me to get Bridgett here on time and I will see you later."

Adam stepped onto the front porch full of uncertainty. Here he had accomplished so much in his life and regretted the majority of it and Bridgett wanted to accomplish something…anything. The difference was Bridgett's future accomplishments would be honest.

Not that any of Adam's music was a farce. They were all legitimate musicians, wrote their own songs and performed live without the aid of any pre-recorded tracks. But the angrier he'd gotten, the angrier their music had become. Sales had begun to dwindle and where they'd once headlined their own tours, they'd had to co-headline in order to sell tickets during this last run.

At the end of the day, Adam still loved music. It was his passion, but he wanted to use it to guide people, especially kids, down the right path. If he had to be the poster boy for what not to do in the music industry, so be it. He wanted people to learn from his mistakes. He wondered if he should write a book about the things he'd gone through, lessons he'd learned. Maybe he could donate the proceeds to a worthy cause.

When he'd originally sketched his music school, he had assumed it would be in LA. The potential for success was high and he'd done a substantial amount of preliminary research. Now he pictured the school in Texas, allowing those who didn't have access to the recording metropolises to learn and grow with their music. He wasn't sure if it would be Katy, Ramblewood or somewhere in between, but he'd decided Texas was best.

He wanted desperately to share his ideas with Bridgett and wondered if it were possible without her linking the pieces together. His biggest fear would be if she asked him to play something for her at the music store next to The Magpie. Too risky. She would be sure to recognize his voice then. It would have to wait.

Adam wanted to make Bridgett's birthday special without overwhelming her. He'd love to write her a song, knowing she'd appreciate the sentiment, but he'd have to save that idea for next year. *Next year.* The thought of a future with Bridgett easily slipped into his thoughts. Adam snipped a rose from the side of the Bed & Biscuit, and decided to drop by the The Magpie to wish Bridgett a happy birthday. An idea for a present came to mind, one he was positive she'd love. He tabled any thought of telling Bridgett the truth today. This was her day and it deserved to be special.

"HAPPY BIRTHDAY!"

Maggie, Bert and Lark startled Bridgett with a mini celebration when she entered the luncheonette's kitchen. They gathered around a chocolate ganache cake—her favorite—a single lit candle glowing in its center.

"Before you say anything, I know you wanted a low-key birthday," Maggie began. "But we refuse to let this day go by without acknowledging how much we love you and how important you are to us. Besides, I only make this cake for special occasions and I can't think of a more perfect reason than your birthday."

Tears welled in Bridgett's eyes, and her breath hitched in her throat, rendering her unable to speak. She managed a nod and hugged her dear friend.

"Happy birthday, kiddo." Bert cut in and wrapped his arms around her. "I may never have had any children of my own, but if I had a daughter, I'd want her to be just like you. I love you as if you were my own."

Oh, that did it. Bring on the ugly-cry face.

"Look what you two have done to her." Lark passed Bridgett a wad of paper towels. "We don't know each other very well, but since the day I arrived, you have been nothing but nice to me. Thank you for being one of my first friends in town. Happy birthday."

"Thank you." Lark's non-sappy diversion allowed Bridgett an opportunity to compose herself. "Thank you all. This was sweet of you. I normally don't have chocolate cake for breakfast, but today I am definitely making an exception. Who's up for a slice?"

"Blow out your candle before it burns the cake," Maggie said. "Make a wish and don't give me any arguments."

Bridgett knew birthday wishes were a frivolous superstition, but she'd thought that about love at first sight, too, and now she questioned the possibility. Bridgett wished for the only thing she really wanted. Happiness—hopefully with Adam—somewhere drama free, and blew out the candles. Despite wanting to leave town and start over, Bridgett loved the people she worked with. Possibly too much to ever be able to leave them.

The four of them gathered in the kitchen, eating, while Bert and Maggie shared embarrassing stories about Bridgett's childhood.

"Lark, you should've heard her." Maggie waved her fork. "She couldn't have been much more than five at the time. She burst into the luncheonette, climbed on a chair and belted out the song '9 to 5' at the top of her lungs." Maggie imitated a young Bridgett standing with her legs apart, hands on hips and her chest puffed out. "I have no idea how she got it in her head to come over here on her own, but she sure made a grand entrance."

Lark stared at Bridgett. "Did you want to be a singer?"

"At that age, I thought I could be the next Dolly Parton," Bridgett snickered. "My boobs didn't quite measure up. But I can carry a tune—in the car with the windows rolled up."

The front bell jangled. Maggie peered through the pass-through window, smiling. "Our first customer of the morning. Bridgett, dear, would you mind?"

"Um, yeah." Bridgett rested her plate on the stainless steel counter and exited the kitchen. "Welcome to—"

Adam stood near the luncheonette's entrance holding a single pink rose.

"Happy birthday! Did you think I wouldn't find out?" Adam crossed the narrow dining area and gave Bridgett a chaste kiss on the cheek. "I'll give you a better one later when we don't have an audience," Adam whispered, handing Bridgett the rose. "This is for you, but don't tell Mazie I raided her rosebush. The florist isn't open yet."

"Thank you and I purposely hadn't mentioned it because I don't want you to fuss over me. It's not—"

Bridgett stopped mid-sentence. Adam stared past her, clearly not listening to a single word she said. Bridgett spun around and caught Lark, Bert and Maggie waving from the kitchen pass-through.

"Okay, what's going on?" Bridgett tapped her foot. "And don't lie. Your smirks and giggles gave you away. What are you trying to rope Adam into?"

"Isn't she paranoid?" Bert shook his head and disappeared from view.

"Are you in on some surprise with them?" Bridgett poked Adam's chest. "Because if you are—"

Adam cut her off with a kiss, breaking it once Bridgett finally relented. "Sorry. I did warn you another kiss was coming. You taste like chocolate."

"Maggie made me a birthday cake." Bridgett's lips still tingled from his kiss. She shied away from him as the first legitimate customer of the morning walked in. "Would you like a slice or are you staying for breakfast?"

"I can't." Adam checked his watch. "I need to take care of a few things before I start my job tomorrow, but I will be here to pick you up after work. We're going pumpkin picking."

Lark waited on the customer allowing Bridgett a few more seconds with Adam. "Pumpkin picking?" She may not have wanted anyone to go out of their way for her birthday, but traipsing through a muddy field wasn't exactly what she had in mind, either. "Good thing I keep a spare change of clothes here. Why the sudden urge to visit the pumpkin patch?"

"Mazie asked if I'd do her a favor. She's afraid they'll run out of good pumpkins by the weekend, I guess. She's too busy to do it herself and said you'd know the sizes she normally uses."

"Uh-huh." Bridgett smiled. Classic Mazie—good excuses had never been her forte. "Translation…she wants you to keep me occupied after work. What's really going on?" The fact that her friend ignored her *don't plan anything* request warmed Bridgett. Knowing her friends cared had lightened the dreariness of the past few weeks.

Adam shook his head. "The truth is, if you head straight to the inn you'll insist on working. Mazie would rather see you enjoy some time off on your birthday. And that means pumpkin picking with me. Besides, I haven't been since I was a kid and I'm looking forward to it."

"If you say so." Bridgett pressed her palms together. "Promise this isn't a trick to get me to Slater's Mill tonight."

"It's not." Adam began to reach for her when another customer entered. "I understand why you don't want to go. We'll talk later."

Bridgett quickly hugged him goodbye. "Thank you for the rose and for stopping in." Bridgett watched Adam's retreating backside. She always did love a man in snug-fitting jeans and Adam's highlighted what the good Lord gave him. That was a little birthday gift she'd keep to herself.

The rest of the morning went surprisingly smoothly considering Bridgett had fully expected her mother, Darren or Abby to wander in. Fortunately, they stayed away. Thanks to the party at Slater's Mill, the majority of the customers knew it was her birthday. She really didn't mind. In fact, she rather enjoyed it. She was surprised by the number of people who took time out of their busy schedules to stop by and wish her well.

A hint of guilt nagged at her for dismissing tonight's celebration. She hadn't meant to appear ungrateful or to hurt Abby's feelings, but she wasn't in the mood for the entire town to witness a reunion between four estranged family members. It was difficult enough dealing with them individually…in private. They may live relatively close to one another, but they weren't a big happy family.

Regardless of her mother's reasons, the pity people showed toward Bridgett ate away at her. The few occasions she'd been to Slater's Mill since the whole twin revelation, the stares and whispers had caused her to slip out the side exit. Eventually it would die down. She just needed to remain patient and keep her distance from public events. And the instant a job offer came in she'd put even more distance between herself and the whole mess. Well, that *had* been her plan until Adam showed up.

Bridgett dropped off a load of dirty dishes in the kitchen and could've sworn she heard Adam's voice by the back door. As she moved closer, Bert began coughing loudly, causing Maggie to pop her head in from outside. Ducking out of view for a second, Maggie reappeared, physically guarding the exit.

"I won't even ask because you won't tell me anyway." Bridgett walked away.

When her shift ended, she couldn't wait to see Adam. The simplicity of an afternoon picking pumpkins had its appeal. It would keep her mind from drifting to the sad realization that, for the first time in her life, she wouldn't see her mom on her birthday. Bridgett's mood lifted the instant Adam braked in front of the luncheonette. She scampered into the truck beside him, practically landing on his lap. She attacked him with a passionate kiss, silently singing "Happy Birthday to Me".

"Where did that come from?" Adam struggled to resume his normal breathing.

"I figured since no one was watching why not take advantage of the situation. After today, I won't see you as much." She winced at the thought. Almost a week had passed, and she'd enjoyed living down the hall from Adam. She hoped he'd still want to see her once he moved onto the ranch. It was convenient at the Bed & Biscuit. The ranch would require effort on his part because her car probably wouldn't survive too many trips.

"Ah, you're taking advantage of me." Adam smiled. "I see how it is."

"You have no idea." Bridgett's hand trailed down his chest and across his flat stomach. "Are you sure you want to stay in Ramblewood? Wouldn't you like to take a long drive out to California, dip your toes in the Pacific and leisurely return by way of New York?"

California. Adam interwove his fingers with hers before he lost sight of his senses. The idea of a cross-country trip with Bridgett tempted him, but the mention of California set his teeth on edge. "Honey, let's see how things go first, then once I'm more settled and have some time off work we'll talk about a trip."

"If it's about money, I'm willing to pay for ha—"

"It's not about money." Adam released her. They could travel to a new place every day and never want for anything. He could give Bridgett the ultimate birthday gift…the freedom to see the world and escape the town she so desperately wanted to put behind her. It would also create a larger gap between Bridgett and her family. He'd much rather see them work it out than have her go through his personal brand of hell.

Only the truth stood between them. Lying to Bridgett caused his heartbeat to grind to a halt. He wasn't proud of himself. But if he told her the truth, this very moment, and she ran, he'd always wonder *what if.* And if he told her the truth and she stayed, he'd wonder if it was because he was the easiest way out of Ramblewood. But those choices robbed him of the one thing he selfishly wanted—a chance to begin again. He could offer Bridgett a fresh start, or take his own. The risk of losing her was too great. As much as Adam hated deceiving her, he'd hate losing Bridgett more. He'd tell her and everyone the truth once he proved his worth. Maybe by then people would see him as Adam Steele. Not The Snake.

Bridgett slid to the passenger side of the cab and flopped against the seat. "Fine, I get it."

Adam raked his hand through his hair. "No, you don't. I have money. It's not—"

"Well, good for you." Bridgett's hand hovered above the door handle. "I watch every penny. I'll probably have to spend a good chunk of my savings on a new car soon. And once I spend it, it'll take years before I can save it again. Enjoy *your money*, but please don't tell me it's not about the money, because if I had some of it, I'd be long gone from here."

Adam reached for her before she opened the door. "Please don't leave. I'm sorry." Bridgett's fingers eased from the handle and Adam feared his next words would push her further away. "Family is more important than anything else. Trust me, Bridgett. I'm getting nowhere with my family and it kills me to see yours desperately trying to have a relationship with you. Be careful what you wish for. Some families go away and never come back."

BRIDGETT HADN'T REALIZED how much his family's rejection had hurt Adam until this moment. She knew it bothered him, but the magnitude of the situation hadn't hit her until now. She wasn't sure how she'd feel if her mother or even Abby refused to talk to her. But wasn't that what she was doing to them?

Bridgett groaned. "I am so sorry. I've been completely insensitive about your family. I can only imagine what you must think of the way I'm acting toward mine."

Adam drew her close to his side. "I understand the

betrayal you're feeling. I just wanted you to see it from another point of view."

"I do," Bridgett whispered as his mouth sought hers. Adam gently brushed her hair aside and tilted her head back, trailing kisses down the side of her neck.

He lifted his head, his breath ragged. "Will you please show me where this pumpkin patch is before we find ourselves in a whole heap of trouble?" Adam slid back to the driver's seat and shifted the truck into Reverse, easing out of the parking space. "I don't think the Ramblewood police would appreciate us making love right here on Main Street."

"I still can't quite figure you out." Bridgett studied him. "I sense a wild and reckless cowboy on the outside and this total family man hovering under the surface. I'm not sure what to think."

Adam stiffened. Had she offended him? Maintaining his focus on the road, Adam didn't acknowledge the comment.

"I don't mean it in a bad way." Bridgett saw the tension ease from his shoulders slightly. Friendships came naturally to Bridgett…romantic relationships did not. She tidied her ponytail from their mini-makeout session, relieved when she caught Adam smiling at her. "I guess this is new to the both of us and we're still trying to figure one another out. I bet you have questions about me, too."

"Another reason why I think a trip should wait. Not because I question my feelings for you."

"How do you feel?" Bridgett held her breath, waiting for his response.

"My grandfather used to tell us the story of when he fell in love with my grandmother. It happened the day they met, at a train station in Missouri. I couldn't fathom how someone could possibly know they were in love so quickly. But I'm beginning to understand it. I think I can safely say, as long as you are in Ramblewood, I will be, too. No matter what happens with my family. And I hope you'll reconsider leaving town if any of those places you've applied to offer you a job. I'd hate to see us end before we begin."

Bridgett's thoughts had a difficult time keeping pace with her frenzied heartbeat. Those words were better than any birthday present she ever could've received.

Chapter Six

"Surprise!"

"I am going to kill you." Bridgett turned and punched Adam in the arm. "I specifically asked you if Mazie had planned a party and you feigned innocence. I won't trust you again."

"Happy birthday, girlfriend." Lexi gave Bridgett a smothering hug. "You didn't think we'd let your birthday go by and not celebrate it, did you?"

Lexi released Bridgett just long enough for Shane to squeeze in and give her a hug.

"I half expected Mazie to pull some sort of stunt, but I never imagined you two would be here. Especially you, Shane."

"When have I ever missed your birthday? And if I did, it was only because I was on the rodeo circuit," Shane said. "Today's *your* special day."

Bridgett appreciated Shane's subtle emphasis.

"The four of you are amazing. Thank you." Bridgett bit back her tears and faced Adam. "I knew I heard you out behind The Magpie talking with Maggie earlier. It was about this, wasn't it?"

"In a matter of speaking," Adam smiled. "They wanted to make sure you weren't late for your own party."

"Instead, Mazie ensured I'd rummage through a muddy pumpkin patch so I'd arrive filthy." Bridgett attempted to grab Mazie with her dirty hands. "How can I thank you?"

"You'll always look beautiful to me," Adam said. A collective *aww* came from the other side of the room.

"Save the sugar for dessert. I need a minute to clean up. I'll be back." Bridgett hurried up the newly carpeted staircase.

"So do I." Adam began to follow her up the stairs.

"Hold it, cowboy," Shane called to Adam.

Adam stopped midstep and faced the dining room.

"What did I do wrong?" Adam asked.

"If you go up there, we won't see the two of you for the rest of the night," Shane laughed. "You can wash up down here. We'd appreciate celebrating Bridgett's birthday with her before you two celebrate privately."

Safely at the top of the staircase, Bridgett felt the warmth of a blush flood her cheeks. She'd had her share of boyfriends in her teens and early twenties—some might say more than her share—but none of her friends had teased her this warmly about one before.

After a quick change of clothes, Bridgett rejoined them in the dining room. Mazie had prepared Bridgett's favorite Andouille sausage Cajun jambalaya. After dinner and a few bottles of wine, Mazie brought out Bridgett's second birthday cake of the day. Homemade

French lemon cake topped with fresh whipped cream—the highlight of the meal.

"Mazie, you've outdone yourself," Bridgett said in between mouthfuls.

"I'm sorry, honey," Shane said to Lexi. "I'm moving in here and you can run the ranch…I could handle a dinner like this every night."

"Since when isn't Hamburger Helper good enough for you?" Hands on hips, Lexi playfully glowered at Shane. "I have no business in the kitchen just as you wouldn't want Mazie around the business end of a horse."

"Lexi does have a point," Mazie chimed in.

"This lemon cake is the best I've had anywhere in the world," Adam said.

"Have you traveled extensively?" Lexi asked.

Adam seemed to linger while wiping his mouth with his napkin before he answered. "I traveled with friends not long ago."

He didn't expand on who the friends were or where they'd gone. Bridgett wondered if by *friends* he meant an ex-girlfriend. She'd half hoped somebody would ask him more questions, but for once the chattering trio remained silent.

"More coffee?" Mazie asked.

"In a minute," Lexi said. "I want to give Bridgett her present."

"Lexi, I told you not to," Bridgett protested. "Dinner with you four is gift enough."

"Will you hush up, please?" Lexi excused herself from the table and disappeared into the kitchen, returning with a small box wrapped in zebra-striped paper and a turquoise bow. "Happy birthday, my friend."

Bridgett smiled at the package Lexi set before her. "This is definitely a Lexi wrapping job."

Bridgett tugged at the paper, revealing a black velvet box. Lifting the hinged lid, she covered her mouth, shaking her head. "Lexi."

"Don't you start with the tears." Lexi crouched down beside her chair. "You have had your eye on that for as long as I can remember. I knew you would kill me if I bought you a new one, so I'm giving you mine."

"I can't take this. It's been in your family for years." Bridgett ran her fingers over the heavy silver chain and oversize, antique filigree locket. "It's beautiful but it should go to Mazie, not me."

"Lexi and I have already discussed it," Mazie added. "It's perfectly fine with me. You're a part of our family."

"And I want you to have it." Lexi covered Bridgett's hands with her own. "I don't wear it as often as I used to. It's too long for me to wear when I'm working with the horses. Plus Shane gave me a diamond pendant for a wedding gift. This has been sitting in a box for a long time. It deserves to be worn."

"Thank you." She wiped away her tears. The gift of her friend's beloved locket meant more to Bridgett than anyone could've imagined. She'd never owned anything more than cheap flea-market jewelry. The locket was pure silver and over a hundred years old.

"It's very beautiful." Adam leaned closer. "I have a gift for you, too." He excused himself from the table and ran upstairs, returning seconds later. "Happy birthday, and I hope this is the beginning of many more we share together."

As he put the pink-and-silver gift bag on the table before Bridgett, the second collective *aww* of the evening resonated throughout the room.

"Adam, we had this conversation earlier. You shouldn't have."

Adam addressed the table. "Is she always this argumentative?"

"Yes," everyone replied at once.

Bridgett removed the tissue paper from the bag, and lifted out three hand-tooled leather journals in various shades of pink, lilac and baby blue.

"Those are for the recipes you'll use in your future restaurant."

"What a clever idea," Mazie said. "You'll have no problem filling these up. You should see her in the kitchen, Adam."

Bridgett leaned affectionately into him, tilting her face to his for a kiss. "Thank you, for the gift and your faith in me.

"Mazie." Bridgett laid the journals on the table and rose to give her friend a thank-you hug. "This dinner means the world to me. I am truly blessed to have you as a friend, especially after all you've done for me these past few weeks. I love you. I love you all. Family drama aside, this tops my best-birthday list." Her heart sang with the love of her friends. Their unyielding support had kept her grounded for the past few weeks. A wash of sadness gripped her at the thought of leaving them behind when she moved away. Maybe Adam was right.

Maybe she needed to give more thought to moving away from Ramblewood.

"It doesn't have to end yet," Shane said.

Lexi elbowed her husband hard in the ribs, shaking her head.

"It's okay, Lexi," Bridgett said. "I actually feel guilty for not going to Slater's tonight. I guess it wouldn't hurt to poke my head in and say hello. Mom will be there and as much as I said I didn't want to see her, my birthday doesn't feel complete without her."

"Are you sure?" Lexi asked.

"Yes, it will be fine. I can leave if it turns dicey."

"Why don't all of us walk down together?" Adam asked. "Safety in numbers."

"You four go ahead," Mazie said. "I need to clean up before my guests return from dinner."

"I wondered where everyone was." Bridgett began to clear the table.

"Oh, no you don't." Mazie waved Adam to the table. "Take your girlfriend out dancing. No more work for you on your birthday. Maggie told me she gave you the day off and you refused."

Bridgett protested as Adam physically lifted her over his shoulder and carried her to the door. "I hate leaving you. Please join us."

"I have work to do and a business to run." Mazie stacked the plates and silverware into one pile. "Have fun tonight."

Bridgett struggled until Adam put her down. "We won't be back late." Bridgett dashed to the table, gathering her gifts to bring upstairs. She smiled at her friends.

"I think this is definitely the start of a new beginning. I can't wait to see what happens next."

WHEN THEY RETURNED from Slater's Mill, exhaustion began to set in. Bridgett had been quiet at the honky-tonk, but she'd managed a few pleasantries with her mother and sister while maintaining a safe distance from Darren. It wasn't until their walk home a few hours later that she'd become more talkative again.

Saying their goodbyes to Lexi and Shane, Adam and Bridgett climbed the oak staircase to the second floor. Walking Bridgett to her room, Adam hesitated to say good-night. He'd much rather make love to her until the sun rose.

"I had fun tonight," Bridgett whispered. "Thank you for the lovely gifts, I can't wait to start creating new dishes. Hopefully it won't be too long before I open my own restaurant. I get excited just thinking about it."

"Don't ever let go of your dreams, Bridgett." Adam brushed an errant lock of hair from her face.

"I can promise I will fill every page of those journals you gave me. In fact, I'm planning to keep the smaller one in my purse."

"I figured maybe you would, which is why I chose that size for you." Adam wished he could give Bridgett the restaurant she wanted. Maybe one day he'd have the opportunity. "I guess we should call it a night."

"What time do you have to be at the ranch in the morning?" Bridgett asked.

"Six o'clock." He couldn't remember when he'd last started a job so early in the morning. The life of a rock star began at six in the evening. "You'll be off to work before I am."

"Get a good night's sleep, and if I don't see you in the morning, good luck tomorrow. The Langtrys are great people to work for. And as you can already tell, I think of them as my second family."

Adam bent his head and kissed Bridgett softly on the mouth, deepening the intensity to a dangerous level in the hallway. Reluctantly he broke away before he lost the ability to stop.

"You *will* see me before you head to work in the morning," Adam said. "Happy birthday, sweetheart. I meant what I said earlier. I hope today is the beginning of many more we celebrate together."

"I do, too." Bridgett slipped into her bedroom and closed the door, leaving Adam alone in the hallway. The walk back to his room seemed more like a mile than twenty feet.

Once inside, Adam sat on the bed and set his alarm for the morning. Tonight had turned out better than he had anticipated. He pulled out his wallet, making sure he had everything he needed for his first day at work tomorrow. According to his temporary driver's license and registration, he was an official resident of Texas again. Coming back to Texas felt better than he'd thought it would. He didn't need the job at Bridle Dance and anyone who knew him would probably question his sanity for taking it.

Playing guitar in front of thousands of screaming fans had been a fantasy throughout his teen years He'd started playing guitar at twelve. By the age of sixteen, he'd had enough songs to fill a notebook. At twenty, he'd tried his hand at Nashville. He hadn't fared well, but didn't give up. At twenty-three, he was back again. And that's when it had happened. A Los Angeles manager in town with one of his bands saw Adam at The Bluebird Cafe and convinced him to move to California. It was the start of him losing control over his life. The more estranged he'd become from his family, the more he'd partied. What wasn't there to like? He'd had fame, women, fast cars and money.

In the beginning he'd loved being on the road. They'd arrive in a new city, do a little sight-seeing, run a sound check, head to dinner somewhere exotic and expensive, then they'd perform. The adrenaline high that came with a live performance had been dangerously addictive. They'd always wanted more and their agent had been more than happy to book the shows. Adam had been living his dream.

But it had fallen flat once the novelty wore off. Being on tour, singing the same songs night after night, nothing had ever changed. They'd lived in a continuous loop for up to eighteen months at a time. Only the city they performed in changed, and those began to blur after a while. Now shoveling horse manure held more appeal. He needed to feel useful again. He wanted to work with his hands and have a sense of accomplishment at the end of the day.

Standing up, he undressed and let his clothes fall to the floor. He slipped beneath the cool crisp cotton sheets, and immediately wished he had Bridgett by his side. Of course, if she were, they wouldn't be sleeping.

But once they had gotten used to sleeping together, he easily envisioned them holding each other through the night. That was perfection.

"CRAP!" ADAM ROLLED to the edge of the bed and reached for the clock. He must've hit the snooze button on his phone because he had less than thirty minutes to get ready and head to the ranch. Bridgett was long gone at this point.

So much for promising to see her in the morning. He wished she'd knocked on his door to wake him up. Then again, she'd probably reasoned he needed the sleep before his big day. Adam typed a short text message apologizing for missing her before he bolted into the bathroom and took a quick shower.

He enjoyed the relaxing drive to Bridle Dance. He'd driven more in the past week than he probably had in the past year. Between airplanes, limos and tour buses, he rarely had a chance to get out on his own, let alone behind the wheel of a car or truck. The brisk morning breeze wafted through the cab carrying the scent of freshly tilled fields ready for fall planting. Who would've thought the smell of dirt would bring him such a sense of calm.

Early morning fog hovered above the road as he entered the Bridle Dance Ranch. If he owned property this gorgeous, he'd never want to leave it. His family's ranch in Katy was beautiful but couldn't compare to the Langtrys'. Although, Adam had to admit, for a family as wealthy as they were, they didn't flaunt their money.

Adam hoped he'd be able to see more of Dance of

Hope in action during his time on the ranch. He admired their devotion and appreciated why Abby had left Charleston to work at the facility.

Adam knew Bridgett felt inferior to her newfound twin sister. But he didn't think it was really because Abby had more education. Bridgett just hadn't come into her own yet. She'd always lived under someone else's roof, worked for someone else, and she didn't have the financial means her sister did. He supposed moving away would give her the independence she needed, but he worried she would also feel very lonely. He didn't think she realized the difference a tight-knit community and close family could make in someone's life. Material things could only take you so far—he was proof of that.

Once he settled into living in the bunkhouse, getting dirty and developing more than guitar calluses on his hands, he would call his manager and give the approval to move ahead with the press releases. He wanted the chance to prove himself as a man, not only to Bridgett, his family and the rest of Ramblewood, but to himself. He wanted to look in the mirror at the end of the day and respect the man who stared back at him.

Adam parked his truck and met Shane in the ranch offices above the main stables.

"I'll introduce you around up here and then you'll fill out your paperwork." Shane led Adam down a short hallway into a large communal office. "For a ranch this size, our office personnel is on the small side. My father stressed a casual yet professional environment while maintaining the family atmosphere."

Adam's nerves calmed further with each introduction. An overwhelming sense of belonging enveloped him. "I bet your employees appreciate the sentiment."

"I think they do. We strive to be one big happy family. Of course, we have our moments and grate on each other's nerves once in a while, but it won't be long before you know everyone who works here. We're in the process of completing the renovations on the bunkhouse you'll be staying in. Is Saturday good for you?"

"Saturday's perfect." Adam's excitement was marred solely by his disappointment about leaving Bridgett. He'd grown accustomed to living down the hall from her. Now she'd be across town.

"Don't worry." Shane slapped Adam on the back. "Absence makes the heart grow fonder. She'll be itching to see you at the end of the day."

Adam liked Shane. The man was straightforward and fully supported his relationship with Bridgett. Hopefully it stayed that way.

After filling out his employment forms, he sat down with the ranch's accountant, Kenny Gilbert.

"I need to make a copy of your driver's license and your Social Security card for our files, and if you'll jot down the make, model and plate number of your truck I'll get you a sticker for the side window. We tow any unauthorized vehicles and on a ranch this size, you'd be surprised how many teenagers try to sneak down of our back roads in search of a secluded hanky-panky spot."

Adam chuckled at Kenny's reference. The man might be in his late sixties, but Adam easily pictured him as the type to run off and find just such a spot in his day.

"I have my truck information written out for you already." Adam removed a folded piece of paper from his wallet. "I figured you'd need it. And I apologize for the temporary license. I lost mine the other day and motor vehicles gave me a temporary. Once I receive my actual license in the mail, I'll bring it in."

Kenny nodded, and ran Adam's information through the flatbed scanner. "I hear you and Bridgett are an item." Adam silently thanked God when Kenny didn't further question him about his identity. "Sweet kid. My wife says you two make a nice couple."

"Thank you." Adam grinned. He hadn't realized they were the talk of the town.

"Just don't break her heart," Kenny continued. "How's she doing? What a horrible thing for her to have to suffer through. And Darren, I don't blame his wife for moving in with her parents in Oklahoma. Good thing their three kids are grown and living elsewhere. They won't have to endure the garbage Bridgett has. Abby's a cute little thing, though. Great addition to Dance of Hope."

"Bridgett's doing great, better than ever actually." If Adam hadn't already known the details of Bridgett's situation, Kenny had divulged much more than anyone had a right to. No wonder the constant gossip upset Bridgett.

"Glad to hear it." Kenny stood up and held out his hand. "You're finished in here. See Shane about the bunkhouse on Saturday. He'll give you a key when you move in. And welcome to Bridle Dance."

It was official. Adam had transitioned from rock star to ranch hand. Walking through the stables, he longed to take one of the horses out for a ride. He hadn't been in a saddle in over a year, but horsemanship never left your blood. He'd been born into ranching and it was probably where he should have remained. He still could have played guitar, maybe even given lessons. Either way, he wouldn't have lost his family's respect if he had stayed on the ranch and in the family business, just as his father had done. He wouldn't have gotten rich, but he would have been a hell of lot happier.

As much as he wanted to call his family and tell them how he had begun to turn his life around he knew he still had a lot to prove. He'd tell Lizzy, and if she decided to tell them, fine. If not, Adam was all right with waiting. The more time he put in on the ranch, the more respect he'd earn. Anyone could get a job; doing the actual work was the hard part. And Adam was determined to work harder than he ever had before. He belonged back in Texas and God willing he'd live out his days with a good woman by his side. And he had just the woman in mind.

Chapter Seven

"God, I hurt." Adam groaned, easing from his bed. "I need to soak in a hot tub."

If he had still lived in Los Angeles, he would have. Adam was a few days into his new job, but yesterday had been roughest; overnight the pain and stiffness had increased. He needed to loosen up before somebody questioned his "good ol' boy" roots. He definitely couldn't limp like an old man once he moved into the bunkhouse tomorrow. Why had he agreed to take Bridgett dancing at Slater's Mill tonight? Because he couldn't stand to let her down. Maybe he could convince her to cuddle up with him in one of the softly padded booths. He wasn't up for the "Boot Scootin' Boogie" line dance tonight.

Adam had expected to muck horse stalls for the first couple of weeks on the ranch, but instead he and Shane had ridden the fences from sunup to sundown. Even when he'd lived on his parents' ranch, he hadn't put in this much saddle time.

His entire body ached along with his male libido, which he'd squashed twice thanks to a few uncoordinated and poorly positioned mounts in the saddle. Adam had prayed Bridgett wouldn't mistake his lack of physical desire as a sign that he was losing interest in their relationship.

Quite the opposite. They'd hardly spent more than an hour or two together during the past two days. When he'd arrived home from the ranch, they had both been ready to call it a day. Early mornings meant early nights, and that didn't leave much of an opening for dating.

It would all be worth it in the end. At least that's what Adam told himself every night when he climbed into bed alone. If it worked out the way he had intended it to, he'd buy a nice house on a few acres of land in Texas and open his music school. The less time he spent with Bridgett, the more he ached for her. Shane had been right. It had made his heart grow fonder. He blessed modern technology for the ability to send text messages. He would've loved to video-chat with Bridgett but her prepaid phone didn't have those capabilities. He had to keep reminding himself she didn't have access to the luxuries he'd become accustomed to.

Adam's life had changed the moment he'd walked into The Magpie and he'd seen Bridgett for the first time. It still amazed him how his morning had begun horribly that day and ended with so much hope.

That hope brought along an unexpected addition to his plans for the future. After seeing many of his new coworkers with their families on the ranch, Adam had begun to seriously contemplate having kids for the first time in his life.

Adam hobbled into the bathroom and turned on the

shower. Children had never been on his radar before. Outside of a couple of the children's charities the record label had sponsored, he hadn't spent much time around them. He hadn't been sure if he wanted any of his own, but the idea had begun to grow on him. He wondered how he'd do as a father. It'd been difficult enough dealing with four band mates, let alone babies and diapers. But his outlook was changing—he could feel the shifts within himself day by day. The thought of being a husband and a father was starting to grow on him...especially when he looked at Bridgett.

Adam managed to shower and shave before Bridgett left for The Magpie, then headed into the hallway hoping to catch her in the kitchen. After today, he wouldn't be able to send her off to work with a kiss. Instead of the peaceful Bed & Biscuit, he'd wake to the sound of three other men snoring.

Bridgett's door squeaked open. Her lips curled upward the instant she spotted him near the stairs. "Good morning." Bridgett crossed the hallway, reached up and kissed him.

"Good morning." Adam tugged her tighter to his body. The tension he'd felt moments ago eased as her fingers traveled across his chest.

A faint moan emanated from Bridgett. "It's been one week since we first met."

Adam pulled away a bit. "Are we celebrating?" Anniversaries of any sort hadn't particularly meant much to Adam in the past, but maybe it was time to change that, too.

Bridgett's eyes met his, their brightness beginning

to fade. "Not if you don't want to. I meant it feels as if we've known each other for longer. Don't worry, I'm not one of those girly girls who need to celebrate stupid anniversaries."

"They're not stupid." Adam dipped his head for another kiss. "I promise to be back at a reasonable hour tonight so we can head to Slater's…to celebrate. Come on." He reluctantly released her. "I'll drop you off at work on my way to the ranch."

No matter what it took, Adam realized, he wanted to remind Bridgett of their first meeting forty-nine years and fifty-one weeks from today. Nothing would stop them from staying together. Not even his past.

"JUST A HEADS-UP," Lark began as Bridgett walked behind the lunch counter. "Your mom called in a to-go order."

A week ago, knowing her mother would be stopping by would've bothered Bridgett. She'd asked Ruby to give her space and her mom had respected the request. Of course, it also gave her mother guilt-free time to spend with her new daughter, but that was okay, too. The two of them needed to get to know each other better anyway. Bridgett shook her head. Somewhere over the course of the past week, she'd actually accepted her mother's relationship with Abby. If the situation had been reversed, she would have wanted the time alone with her biological mom.

She might feel differently after seeing them together at a family function. She'd have that opportunity soon enough. Thanksgiving was a month away and Abby and Clay's families had planned a huge Thanksgiving dinner as a pre-wedding party. Clay's family had hosting duties and his mother had personally invited Bridgett and Ruby.

Somehow, Abby had ended up with a *full house* of parents—three fathers and two mothers. Bridgett had a short hand. Her mother, with her bouffant-styled candy-apple-red hair, bearing a striking resemblance to the Queen of Hearts, and a joker of a father. Bridgett cringed. She hoped Darren hadn't been invited to Thanksgiving dinner, too. Knowing Clay's parents' generosity, he probably had been.

"Thanks for letting me know," Bridgett said to Lark. "I'm okay."

"Are you sure? I don't have to go on break right now. You can head to lunch first and I'll take care of the order."

"Lark, I'm fine," Bridgett reassured her friend. The woman she once thought appeared to be running from something had fast become a good friend. She still caught Lark looking out the window as if she anticipated someone's arrival, but not nearly as often as she had when she'd first come to Ramblewood. "Enjoy your lunch."

Lark hesitated at the door when Ruby walked in, but Bridgett waved her hand, urging Lark to continue on.

"Mom, your order won't be ready for another ten minutes." Bridgett totaled the bill on the cash register.

"Can we talk?" Her mother's usual sing-song voice had faded to a meager plea.

Bridgett shook her head. "Not when I'm working.

I refuse to give the people of Ramblewood anything more to gossip about."

The entire luncheonette had gone silent and she cursed herself for not taking Lark up on her offer. This situation was exactly what Bridgett wanted to avoid.

"Order up!" Bert shouted from the kitchen and slammed his hand down on the silver bell. The sound resonated throughout the small restaurant. Bridgett turned to see Bert standing behind the pass-through window holding up two white takeout bags. He narrowed his eyes in Ruby's direction and thrust the bags toward Bridgett. "We wouldn't want to keep your customer waiting."

Bridgett mouthed a silent thank-you to the man and placed the bags on the counter. She quickly took Ruby's money and handed her back the change.

"I will stop by the salon after work. I can't stay long and I have plans I don't intend to change."

"Plans with Adam?" Ruby asked.

"Mom, we will talk later." Bridgett lowered her voice an octave. "I promise I will be there."

Ruby left without another word and the remainder of the customers went back to their normal chatter. Her head began to throb and when Lark returned from her lunch break, Bridgett was more than ready to escape for a half hour. After a long walk in the park, she plowed through the rest of the day, which went quicker than she'd thought possible. Why was it whenever you dreaded something, it came upon you before you knew it? Yet, when it was something you really wanted—say spending a little alone time with your boyfriend—the day seemed to drag on forever.

"Do you have plans with Adam tonight?" Lark asked as they locked the luncheonette's front door from the outside.

"We're supposed to go to Slater's. I won't hold him to it, though." Bridgett sighed. "He's been coming in really late. I guess he's trying to make a good impression at his new job. But he moves into the bunkhouse tomorrow, so this sort of feels like our last night together. I can't wait to see him…but before I do anything, I need to swing by the salon and see what my mom wants."

"Good luck," Lark said. "No matter what she says, don't let it bring you down. You've been so much happier and relaxed this past week with Adam around. I'd hate to see you retreat into a depressing funk again."

"You and me both." Bridgett faced the salon across the street. "Here goes nothing. I'll see you in the morning."

Entering the Curl Up & Dye Salon sent a chill down her spine. She hadn't returned since the night her mother and Clay had asked her and Abby to meet them there. The night their lives had changed. The salon's pink giraffe-print ceiling and sherbet-striped walls adorned with dozens of round mirrors in various sizes created an eclectic atmosphere. The sleek black styling chairs and frosted-glass manicure stations added a touch of sophistication. Today the salon was packed with customers in various stages of hair and nail treatments.

"Welcome to Curl Up & Dye, where we beautify until you're satisfied," Kylie sang from behind the counter before she even looked up, her hair in an extremely voluminous updo today. "Oh, hey, Bridgett. Ruby hadn't mentioned you were stopping by."

Ruby glided across the salon in her leather pants and thigh-high boots. Only a few months ago she'd been suffering with chronic pain, but now her limp was virtually undetectable thanks to daily physical therapy with Abby.

"Hello, sweetheart." Ruby pulled her daughter into a suffocating hug. Her mother's death grip, combined with too much perfume, made Bridgett wonder if Ruby was trying to kill her or welcome her.

"Why don't we go into my office where it's more private?" Dread set in and Bridgett almost reached out to stop her mother. She had to pick her poison. A brief public conversation sure to spread through town in a matter of minutes or a gut-wrenching private conversation sure to require tissues. They were both dim prospects.

"What's with Kylie's hair?" Bridgett snuck another look over her shoulder, hoping it would lighten the mood. "It's so big and glittery."

"One of the girls was practicing her wedding updos today and Kylie was the guinea pig."

"What's the theme of the wedding?" Bridgett asked. "Attack of the killer beehive?"

"I told her it was too much." Ruby laughed. "But it's her area of expertise. If the clients are okay with it, I am, too."

Bridgett sat in the chair across from her mother. Neither one of them spoke.

"Well, Mom?" Bridgett leaned forward. "I'm here. What did you want to talk about?"

Ruby tilted her head to one side. "You seem different."

Bridgett sighed. *Here we go with the Ruby theatrics.* "Mom, I'm exactly the same as I was last week, and the week before that. My hair hasn't changed, my clothes haven't changed, nothing has changed."

"You're glowing," Ruby said, turning her head slightly, studying Bridgett further.

"It's called grease." Bridgett stood and grabbed a tissue off her mother's desk, wiping at her face. "I worked in the kitchen most of the morning."

"Are you pregnant?" Ruby asked as if it was the most normal question to ask her daughter in the middle of the afternoon.

Bridgett closed her eyes and tried to formulate a non-sarcastic answer. "No, I'm not. Why am I here?"

"Are you sure?" Ruby reached for her daughter. "If you're not practicing safe sex, you know the risk you're taking."

Oh, that did it. "You would know, because having an affair with a married man and getting pregnant makes you an expert."

Ruby's head jerked sideways as if Bridgett had physically slapped her across the face.

"That was harsh."

"I'm sorry. Yes, it was. This is why I avoided the situation." Bridgett walked to the office door. "Mom, just for the record I don't blame you for getting pregnant with Darren's baby, excuse me, babies. I blame Darren. He was a much older married man who knew better. I'm not even sure if it's fair of me to blame you for separating Abby and me at birth. The jury's still out on that one. But until I can figure it out, these conversations are not healthy for either one of us because we end up hurting each other. I don't want that."

Ruby stood, wringing her perfectly manicured hands. "How do we work through it then?"

"Let it come naturally." The pain in her mother's eyes gripped Bridgett's heart like a vise. "You've done remarkably well at giving me my space these past few weeks and I thank you. I'm still hurt and angry, but not as much as when this first happened. Maybe I'll see it your way one day. Can you accept that and promise not to force it? We need to take it day by day."

"I don't like it, but yes, I can." Ruby dropped her arms to her sides and shifted away from the door. "I'll be here when you're ready."

Bridgett stepped into the hallway, spun around and gave her mother a hug. "I love you, Mom. That hasn't changed."

"I love you, too, honey." Tears ran down Ruby's face, taking her mascara and eyeliner with it.

Bridgett swiped at her mother's tears with her thumb. "I have to go. I have a cooking lesson with Mazie before my date with Adam tonight."

Ruby dabbed at her makeup. "I'm sorry I couldn't afford to send you to Le Cordon Bleu with Mazie."

"It wasn't what I wanted anyway." Bridgett grabbed a tissue for herself. "You did the best you could, struggling to provide for me and growing this business. I have a lot of respect for you. But how you did it alone is beyond me. And that's why I'm furious with Darren. You shouldn't have had to do it alone. You were entitled to child support. I don't understand why you let him get away with it."

"Do you realize how embarrassing it would've been?" Ruby asked.

"Embarrassing for who? You? I'd think it would've been more embarrassing for the married man who cheated on his wife and kids."

"He wants to see you." Ruby shuffled her feet.

"Maybe I'll want to see him, too, but not now."

"Abby on the—"

Bridgett held up her hands. "We're talking about me, not Abby. I have to focus on myself. I don't know what the future holds. I don't even know if I'm going to stay in Ramblewood."

"You're thinking of leaving?" Her mother's complexion paled. "With Adam?"

Bridgett shook her head. "In theory it sounds wonderful, but he's a ranch hand, mom. I can't ask him to spend all his money on an apartment with me. Room and board is part of his pay, take it away and I have no idea how much of a paycheck he's really left with at the end of the week. I might as well tell you...I've been contemplating leaving Ramblewood since the night you told me the truth. I want a fresh start where no one has heard of me. It might be a little difficult with Darren's media coverage, but I'm willing to try."

Bridgett had expected her mother to ask her to stay. Instead, she remained silent. Her shoulders slumped forward with resignation, the fight completely gone. She'd seen her mother through rough times in the past, but she hadn't looked this physically dejected before. It frightened Bridgett.

"Are you still seeing the owner of the movie theatre?" Her mother had sworn there was nothing going on, but Bridgett knew better.

"I haven't been to the movies in a few weeks." Her mother turned quickly, facing her desk and grabbing another tissue. "I've been spending time with Darren lately." The words were barely audible.

Bridgett's knees buckled, and she steadied herself against the filing cabinet. "Mom, no. He's still married."

"We're not having sex." Ruby faced her daughter.

Bridgett squeezed her eyes tightly. "Please stop. Too much information, Mom. I—I really need to go." Bridgett gave Ruby one final hug and dashed out the salon's rear exit to avoid the salon patrons' watchful gazes. Her mother and Darren? Correction. Her mother and her father were seeing each other. The thought left an acrid taste in her mouth.

Running across the street, Bridgett pushed open the iron gate leading to the Bed & Biscuit walkway. Realizing it hadn't made its usual heavy clank behind her, she stopped at the base of the porch stairs and spun around.

"Adam!" Bridgett jumped into his arms. "You have no idea how much I needed to see you."

"Didn't you hear me calling you from across the street?" Adam gave her a quick kiss and stepped back, looking at her carefully. "It was all I could do to keep up with you. I saw you run out of the salon. What's wrong?"

"Mom wanted to talk, which went better than I had

anticipated. She agreed to continue to give me space and then she told me she's seeing Darren."

Bridgett wondered if she'd looked as stunned as Adam when she'd heard the news. He snapped his mouth shut, closed the distance between them and gathered her into his arms. His mouth claimed hers in a deep, passionate kiss. Pulling back slightly, he ran his hands up and down her arms. "I'm sorry."

Bridgett shook her head in dismay. "Let's not talk about it right now. What are you doing here so early?"

"Shane sent me to pick up an order from the Feed & Grain. And I wasn't about to pass up the opportunity to kiss you."

"I can't wait till tonight, and please tell me you don't have to work too late tomorrow. It's Halloween, and Lawson's Farm puts on an incredible show. I really want to go with you."

"Need me to protect you in the haunted maze?" Adam's fingers drifted over her collar bone. "Afraid a vampire bat will bite you."

Bridgett shivered against his touch. "Stop that. You're giving me goose bumps." She giggled. "You're never too old for a Lawson Halloween haunting."

"I think I can swing protecting my girl from ghosts and ghouls." Bridgett swatted his hands away. "I need to get back to the ranch, though. See you later?"

"Are you sure you have time for me tonight?" Bridgett fingered the buttons on his shirt.

"I'll make time." Adam's expression stilled, becoming more serious. "There's no place I'd rather be than with you."

Chapter Eight

The following night Adam wasn't sure if he should be frightened or horrified by the hayride they'd just left. He was still trying to figure out how they'd pulled off the headless horseman. He thought the horse was Shane's, but the rider had been far too short. The worst part had been its eerie resemblance to one of his shows. An "Alice Cooper meets Lizzie Borden" vibe. Although having just been chased with a chainsaw in the middle of the night left little to be desired. Whether it was real or not, it sent his pulse soaring.

Adam's phone rang. Roman. He'd given his new number out to only three people from his old life. Lizzy, Phil and Roman.

"Happy Halloween," Adam answered, distancing himself from Bridgett and the Lawsons so they wouldn't overhear his conversation.

"I hope you're enjoying yourself in Texas because it's hitting the fan here."

Adam felt as if his heart had stopped beating. "What do you mean? And how did you know I was in Texas?"

"Phil told me. And have you checked out TMZ lately?"

Roman's irritation bit through the phone. "During a radio interview this afternoon, JP announced the band had broken up, and according to reputable sources—brace yourself—you're in rehab for every addiction the tabloids have ever claimed."

"I'm in what?" Adam shouted, attracting Bridgett's attention from across the field. He waved and lowered his voice. "What the hell is my family going to think? They might actually believe it this time."

Not that this was any different from ninety percent of the stories the so-called media tossed his way.

"It gets better." Roman cleared his throat. "They say you're in rehab in Texas."

"What the hell? Who goes to rehab in Texas?" Adam felt his shirt begin to cling to his body. "Where in Texas?"

"San Antonio."

Adam exhaled loudly. "It's not exactly the next town over, but it's close enough. When they don't find me, the paparazzi will hit the neighboring towns. Can't you release a statement for me? Divert them far away from here. Confirm the band breaking up part, but deny rehab. Tell them I am off hiking somewhere in Ecuador or…I don't care where. Better yet, have one of the body doubles we used in Japan to divert the fan-mobs photographed in the Australian outback. Sell it to the media. No paparazzo will trek through that terrain to find me."

"Then how am I going to explain the supposed photograph of you?"

"What, I have to do your job for you?" Adam's hand trembled. "Say a tourist took it. Don't make it too per-

fect. Put my publicist on it." Bridgett caught his attention out of the corner of his eye. "I have to go. Text me
when you have something. I can't talk when I'm at the
bunkhouse. Too many people around."

"Why are you living in a bunkhouse anyway? You
can afford to buy any house in the world."

Adam took a deep breath in an attempt to steady his
nerves. "It's not about the money, it's about rebuilding
my life. You wouldn't understand. I have to go."

Adam hung up the phone before Roman had a chance
to answer him. He had faith his manager would handle it. But he'd wished his team had been more proac-
tive instead of reactive. Of course, that was his own
fault. If he'd issued a press release as soon as their tour
ended, none of this would have happened. Instead he
had decided to wait for the right time and now his lies
had begun to snowball. He needed a better grip on the
situation. He also needed to stay away from the center
of Ramblewood. On Bridle Dance he was safe from
the prying eyes. He'd promised to take Bridgett to the
Halloween party at Slater's Mill tonight, but he should
probably stay home and lie low. Would wearing a mask
fool the paparazzi?

"What's wrong?" Bridgett asked. The worry etched
into her brow was visible in the moon's glow. "You
seemed upset on the phone."

Adam had repeatedly told himself he wasn't lying
to Bridgett. He had just purposely left out a portion of
the truth. But that didn't make him any more honest,
and the longer this ruse continued, the deeper he dug

his own grave. "It was just news I didn't want to hear. It will work out in the end."

"You're not leaving, are you?" Bridgett tilted her head, studying him. "You don't look good."

"I'm not leaving." Adam entwined his fingers with Bridgett's. "I have an idea. Instead of going to the Halloween party tonight, why don't we pack a midnight picnic and take a drive." Maybe if he had her alone, the truth would come easier.

"I'd love to, but I have to be at the luncheonette by three in the morning to prepare for catering the police chief's retirement party tomorrow. I would have had to cut tonight short anyway."

"When were you planning on telling me?"

Bridgett fiddled with the frayed waistband on her denim jacket. "It's been a few days since we spent time together, and I hoped I'd have the energy to stay out. But I'm wiped. Between the Halloween orders and the retirement party, Maggie and I have spent the past few days decorating a thousand cupcakes, twenty sheet cakes, and we still have to prepare a full dinner and dessert menu for the chief. It's extra money, though, and I'm grateful for it. It will help me afford an apartment and a new car. Well, a new used car."

"An apartment?" Adam hadn't thought of Bridgett moving out of the Bed & Biscuit. "Where are you moving to?"

"I'm not sure yet. But a restaurant in San Antonio asked me to come in for an interview. If they hire me, I'd be managing a place similar to The Magpie, only with more employees. My interview's Tuesday afternoon."

"You're really going through with this?" Adam turned, storming to his truck. He'd asked her to stay the other day and she had totally disregarded it.

Bridgett scrambled to keep up with him. "Why are you so surprised? I told you from the beginning I planned on leaving town. No one here is hiring for the position or salary I'm looking for. I'll need to make a lot more money to buy my own restaurant."

Adam opened the truck door and then slammed it shut. "I figured since you and I had something going on, you'd reconsider. Especially when I told how much I'd hate to see us end before we began."

"I don't want that, either." Bridgett reached for him, but he shrugged out of her grasp. "But I can't put my life on hold forever. I'd already applied for this job before you came to town and I at least have to see whether it's something I want." She looked up at him, her eyes begging him to understand.

"You're not even sure how long you'll stay in Ramblewood," she continued. "Maybe you could move to San Antonio—it's not that far. Plus, you're missing the giant *if* factor. A lot has to fall into place before it happens. I have to get myself there first. My car certainly won't make it and I can't ask Mazie to borrow hers without raising suspicion."

"She knows." Adam dug his boot into the ground. "She told me the day of your birthday. You forgot to clear your browser history and I forget to tell you."

Bridgett pulled her jacket tighter across her chest. "What she must think of me."

"She thinks what you're doing is admirable." Adam

met her eyes, hoping she could see how much he wanted her to stay. "But she'd rather you did it in Ramblewood."

"Defeats the purpose of a fresh start, doesn't it?" Bridgett paced the length of the truck. "I can't do it, Adam. I need to get out of here."

Adam's heart tore in half. Bridgett worked multiple jobs, only one of which she was paid for, and couldn't afford a decent car or an apartment. He busted his ass for a job he didn't need. He could afford to make their lives much more enjoyable if he'd tell her who he was.

"Why don't we move in together?" Adam asked. Bridgett didn't need to know how much he brought home. She wouldn't have to use any of her own money toward the rent, enabling her to buy a car and still save for her restaurant. *What the hell am I thinking?* He couldn't consciously live with Bridgett and continue to hide the truth from her. It was hard enough now, but sleeping with her…creating a home together? No. The whole truth needed to come out and then she could decide if getting a place together was still an option…or if she still wanted anything to do with him. He took a deep breath. "Bridgett, we need to talk."

"Adam, we've only known each other for a week and half." Her laughter had a sharp edge to it. "I may be untraditional in many ways, but I still believe in getting married before moving in with a guy. I'm in no way pressuring you to propose to me. I am enjoying us, and that doesn't have to change if I move away. We're both working crazy schedules anyway, so then why does it matter if I'm here or an hour and a half from here? I need to do this for myself. I *need* a fresh start."

The reality of what she'd said hit Adam square in the jaw. He'd already admitted to himself that he kept the truth from her because he selfishly wanted a fresh start of his own. He understood her drive to make a new life for herself. He wouldn't stand in her way.

"You've made up your mind, haven't you?"

Bridgett nodded. "I told Maggie last week and my mom the other day. Why does it have to affect us?"

Adam jammed his hands in his pockets. His pulse slowed as if it tried to beat through molasses. "I won't ask you to change your mind. You deserve to put yourself first. But leave me out of the equation. It complicates things.

"Are you breaking up with me?" Bridgett's voice shook.

"I just think maybe we should take a break until you figure this out. If you really want a new life, own it. Once you're grounded wherever you go, then we can see where we stand."

"Please take me home." Bridgett climbed in the truck and firmly closed the door, staring rigidly ahead. Sliding in beside her, Adam drove Bridgett back to the Bed & Biscuit in silence.

The truck pulled to the curb, barely stopping before Bridgett hopped out. Without a glance behind her, she ran up the porch stairs and disappeared inside. Adam's chest ached at the possibility of never knowing what they could have had. It wouldn't have been fair to try to talk her out of doing what she desperately wanted. She needed her independence more than she needed him. Once she had it and recognized her own worth, maybe there would be a place for him in her life. Until then, he'd wait.

Adam had his own life to straighten out. After Roman's news tonight, there was nothing preventing him from putting his Los Angeles home on the market—the whole world already thought he was in rehab and soon, hopefully, they'd think he was in Australia. He'd arrange to have the contents packed and put in storage near Katy until he decided what to do with everything. He had no reservations about leaving his old life behind. His true friends, the few he had, would respect that decision. He hoped that when Bridgett figured out where she wanted to be she'd include him, too.

Shifting his truck into Drive, he drove to Bridle Dance, the one place he felt at home. Unless he counted being wrapped in Bridgett's arms. His body burned with regret. He'd miss her...more than he had a right to.

TWO WEEKS HAD passed since Bridgett had seen Adam. From what Lexi told her, he had been putting in eighteen-hour days. She longed to see him, but whenever she drove out to Lexi and Shane's house, she took one of the many other ranch entrance roads to avoid running into him.

She hated how they'd left it Halloween night, but she respected Adam for putting her first. She was beginning to realize having space could be lonely, though. She'd come to miss the daily interaction with her mother, and even though she'd only known Abby for a short time, she missed her, too. Mazie and Maggie were both upset and Adam...she missed him more than she would have imagined.

She'd finally told Lexi her plans, and as much as her friend hated to see her leave, she'd offered Bridgett her complete support. Lexi had loaned Bridgett her car to use for her interviews. She'd gone on five in total. All in San Antonio. And there'd been more qualified applicants for each one.

Bridgett's 1984 Toyota Corolla puttered down the road to Lexi's house, sounding worse by the mile. With one final sputter, it jolted to a stop, quickly becoming engulfed in white smoke. One of the guys from the garage had told her a few weeks ago that it didn't have much time left—he wasn't kidding. She had hoped to find another car before it died, but there'd been slim pickings in her price range.

Bridgett quickly grabbed everything she could from the car, which wasn't much, and moved a safe distance away. She doubted it was on fire, but with the amount of smoke billowing out from under the hood, she didn't want to risk it. She removed her cell phone from her pocket and called Lexi. Fifteen minutes later Adam pulled up alongside her.

"What happened?" Adam jumped from his truck. "Are you all right?"

Bridgett attempted to contain her happiness at his arrival. His skin had tanned from the strong Southern sun, making his features appear more rugged, borderline dangerous. A black Stetson rested on the dash of his truck and Bridgett ached to see him wearing it.

Bridgett swallowed hard, her throat instantly dry. "I am, but Bubba bit the bullet."

"You named your car Bubba?" Adam chuckled.

"My car burps and farts like a Bubba." Bridgett shrugged. "Can you think of a more appropriate name? Let me guess. Lexi called you."

"Close. Lexi called Shane and he called me. Let me pop the hood and take a look." Adam opened her car door and reached for the hood release. "Although with all this steam, you may have blown your radiator. Will Bubba turn over?"

Bridgett shook her head. "Bubba's dead. The radiator's shot, it leaks oil, the pan is smashed in, the exhaust has a hole in it, one of the tie rods is bent and the crankshaft needs to be replaced. It's not worth it. Bubba's had a good run. The car's older than I am."

"I don't think I've ever seen you this feisty before." Adam lifted the hood and fanned away the smoke. "You're running as hot as this engine."

"What do you expect when your man walks out on you, you're working your fingers to the bone to get ahead and your car craps out?"

"At least you're not bitter." Adam smiled the glorious smile she'd fallen for the day they'd met, almost a month ago. And she still fell for it today. "If it's any consolation, I have missed you."

Bridgett's stomach began to flutter. "I've missed you, too."

"How did your interview go?" Adam shielded his eyes from the sun.

"Interviews," Bridgett emphasized. "Not too good. Turns out, I'm not qualified for much. I'm surprised Lexi or Shane didn't tell you."

Adam closed the distance between them and gripped

her shoulders. "You're qualified for many things. You just haven't found your niche."

Bridgett looked up at him. "Are you going kiss me?"

Adam tilted his head, his eyes focused on her mouth. "Is that what you want?" His voice was thick with desire.

"Yes." Bridgett sucked in her bottom lip.

"It won't change anything, Bridgett." His rough, callused fingers gently brushed a windblown wisp of hair from her face. "I refuse to stand in the way of your dreams."

"Those dreams haven't exactly worked out for me." Bridgett gingerly lifted her fingers to his chest, allowing the weight of her palm to settle against his chest. "I told the people I care about my plans. Now whenever I speak I can see them tense, as if I'm about to drop a bomb on them."

"Can you blame them?" Adam's hands trailed down her sides, increasing in pressure as they wound around her. He drew her close to him, his lips inches from hers. "No one wants to see you leave. But they won't stop you, either. We want you to be happy."

Bridgett's chest rose and fell in unison with his. "What if this makes me happy?"

"Then who am I to deny you?" Adam's lips had just grazed hers when sirens startled them.

A fire truck pulled up, a cloud of dust in its wake. Its crew jumped down and ushered Bridgett and Adam away from Bubba.

"Is anyone hurt? Do you need an ambulance?" one of them asked.

Bridgett waved her arms. "I'm fine—we're both fine. My car died, but I didn't call you guys. It's not on fire."

"Someone called it in saying they saw smoke," the firefighter said. "We still need to check it out."

Bridgett turned to Adam. "Care to give me a ride to Lexi and Shane's? I'll need to get someone to tow this out of here."

Adam dramatically bowed and swept his arm toward his truck. "Your chariot awaits."

"That's good because my coach just turned into a pumpkin." Bridgett laughed.

Adam walked her to the passenger side of his truck. "I've missed your laugh."

"I've missed yours, too." Bridgett climbed in. "I heard you've been keeping yourself pretty busy working. How do you like it?"

"It's the best job I've had in years." Adam ran around the front of the truck and hopped in beside her. "For the most part everyone's been very welcoming. A few of the old-timers are a little set in their ways, but I really have no complaints."

"Anything new with your family?" Bridgett asked.

Adam steered past the fire truck. "Status quo. I still have no intention of moving back to Katy, if that's what you're wondering. My sister's had nothing new to report. She's glad I'm settling in here, though. Since we're on the topic of family, and I swore I wouldn't get involved, but I do see Abby on the ranch. She wants a relationship with you. She's a bit hurt that her twin sister goes out of her way to avoid her."

"You've spoken to her about me?" The thought unsettled Bridgett.

"I haven't told her anything you asked me not to." Adam rested a reassuring hand on Bridgett's thigh. "Abby did the talking…and can she talk. I am in a unique situation. I'm asking my family to give me a second chance and I've had your support the entire time. Abby's also asking for a second chance."

"It's a different situation. I haven't done anything to Abby. Not intentionally. My mother and Darren did. They did it to both of us. It's not the same as your family being mad at you for whatever you did. Outside factors created our mess."

"Does how it started still matter? Your sister is getting married in six weeks and she really wants you to stand up for her. And if you can't do that, you should at least go to the wedding."

"I guess I could call Lexi and ask her to meet me at Dance of Hope instead. It wouldn't kill me to stop in and spend a minute or two with Abby if she's not busy."

"Why don't you and your sister go to dinner tonight? She passes the Bed & Biscuit on the way home. She can drop you off."

"Don't push it, please." She'd agreed to talk with Abby. That was all she was up for at this stage. "What about you? Do you think we could grab dinner one night this week…to talk?"

"I don't want to complicate your life, Bridgett." Adam slowed the truck to a stop at the ranch's entrance. "I'd love to take you to dinner. Hell, I want nothing more than to kiss you, but I told you I'd wait for you to decide what you want."

"Maybe I've already decided." Bridgett shifted in her seat to face him. "I had five interviews in San Antonio. Even if they had turned out, I'm not sure I would have gone for it. I wasn't overwhelmingly thrilled with San Antonio. Don't get me wrong, I love visiting there. It's a beautiful city. But it's a city. With many people. And I can't believe I'm saying this…but it doesn't compare to Ramblewood. After each interview, I found myself itching to get back here. To the people who matter in my life. This is my home—it just took me a while to realize it." Bridgett slid closer to Adam. "And it's your home, too."

Adam hooked his finger under her chin, tilting her face to his. "I'd like nothing more than to build a life here with you." Lowering his mouth to hers, he claimed her lips. The heat from his kiss coursed through her veins. She'd missed his touch. As his strong arms wrapped around her, she knew she'd been a fool to think there was anything better than this out there.

Chapter Nine

The next week and a half flew by at warp speed in Adam's mind. He'd taken the first offer presented to him on the house, much to the delight of his real estate agent, and his attorney had prepared for the closing on Monday. Based on his agent's recommendation, he had hired a mover and they had packed up his house. His belongings were on their way to a warehouse storage center in Texas.

Adam mentally went through the checklist he'd created for his countdown to reveal his true identity, and he had completed every item. His manager and publicist had worked together to compose a series of press releases. Once he told Bridgett the truth, he'd give the go-ahead to issue them.

He could weather whatever the rest of the world threw at him, but he feared Bridgett would never forgive him for deceiving her. They had easily slipped back into each other's lives, and he felt they were on solid footing for once. He hoped when he explained the extent of what he went through to put his old life behind him, it would be enough to prove his sincerity.

But he was fully aware he deserved nothing less than a slap in the face.

"Hey, man." Shane reined his horse to a stop beside Adam and dismounted. "Lexi told me Bridgett's stressed out over this whole Thanksgiving dinner thing tomorrow night with Abby and Clay's families."

"It should be interesting to say the least." Adam crouched down in front of the fence post and checked the soil. "There's a definite leak in the irrigation system along this section. It's rotting the wood away. I'll need to replace these two posts and a couple of rails."

"We repaired a leak here once before." Shane tugged off his gloves. After he phoned the ranch to have someone come out to repair the line, he grabbed a shovel from the bed of the truck and began to dig out the other post. "How are you and Bridgett doing?"

Adam appreciated Shane's work ethic. He could easily have left the job to Adam, but he'd rather do it himself.

"Good." Adam slid a new post off the tailgate. "Having her to myself for the night would be nice, though. Dating is great and all, but the lack of privacy gets old real fast."

Shane jammed his shovel into the muddy soil. "Listen, Lexi and I have a small Airstream travel trailer that we use for weekend escapes. It's way up in the hills alongside a creek. Why don't you take Bridgett and spend the night? It's clean, and I brought out a full tank of propane a week ago."

Adam titled back his hat. "Thank you, I appreciate it.

I'm iffy about how Bridgett will take it, though. I don't want her to think I'm pushing too fast."

"You don't have to spend the night, but the option's available. Pack a dinner, and treat it as a date night. Let what happens happen. I'm sure Bridgett will appreciate a break from the people of Ramblewood and everything that's been happening in her family. Lexi and I had to figure out this blended family thing ourselves not too long ago, and it's not easy. We're a prime example of how a lie gone bad can turn out all right."

"What do you mean a lie gone bad?" Adam asked. Did Shane suspect something about his own situation?

Shane rested his arm on the shovel's handle. "Lexi gave our son Hunter up for adoption. I had no idea I had a son until he was thirteen."

"And your marriage survived?" Adam's lie paled in comparison to Lexi's.

"We weren't married. In fact we were barely a couple. Lexi had Hunter when she was in college. If I hadn't cheated on her and married another woman, I'm sure she would have done things differently."

Adam's mouth went slack. "You cheated on Lexi?"

"It was a one-night stand with a buckle bunny. I was young and foolish. When the woman showed up at my house pregnant, I married her. Turned out the kid wasn't mine and we divorced. When Lexi moved back to town I wanted a second chance. Hunter came into our lives just when we had begun to date again. He ultimately brought us together. I forgave Lexi. I may not agree with how she handled it, but I understand why. I asked her to marry me a few weeks later."

The heaviness in Adam's chest lifted slightly with Shane's personal revelation about his and Lexi's past problems. It confirmed he had made the right decision to come clean with Bridgett and added some much-needed hope and strength to get him through it.

"Lexi's lie changed everything I knew," Shane continued. "But what happened to Bridgett and Abby is much worse. Bridgett's scared and angry and who can blame her?"

"Yeah, I can see why it's so overwhelming for her. Abby's a little tornado, isn't she?" Adam removed two bottles of water from the cooler in the truck's cab and gave one to Shane. "Don't get me wrong, she has a huge heart, but she comes on a bit strong."

Shane twisted the cap off his bottle. "She has the perfect personality for a physical therapist and her determination was exactly what Clay needed to pull him out of his funk. But that's his story to tell. I will say, she took a broken man and made him whole again."

Adam wished Bridgett recognized the similarities between her and her sister. Two strong-willed women, wanting to serve others. Yes, physical therapy was different from wanting to open a restaurant, but people's happiness was the ultimate result of both. One was determined to make the most of their family's situation, and the other was determined to run from it. The sooner Bridgett accepted Abby in her life, the sooner she'd realize she already had the large family she'd once told him she dreamed of.

"You know Bridgett better than I do. How do you

think she'd react if I surprised her with the trailer idea?" Adam asked.

"If you're thinking of blindfolding her and driving her up there, I strongly advise against it." Shane removed his hat, scratching his head. "I'd tell her the truth. That way it's her decision."

"Thank you. You've been an incredible friend." Adam wondered if their friendship would continue once he discovered who Adam was.

"Let's finish this, then you can knock off early." Shane shook the rotted fence post loose. "I'll follow you back, get you the keys and draw you a map. You won't find it without one."

The hair on Adam's arms rose. Was he nervous or excited? Whether they ate dinner and watched the stars, or ended up spending the night together, he'd be happy.

BRIDGETT PARKED THE convertible Mustang Lexi had loaned her alongside Adam's truck at the ranch. With the countless ranch vehicles at Lexi's disposal, she had told Bridgett to keep her car for as long as she needed.

She'd been surprised when Adam had called and mentioned the travel trailer. She had agreed to go there with him but hadn't fully weighed the implications of what the night might bring until she reached Bridle Dance.

She checked her watch. She was almost an hour early. Seeing Barney in the backyard, Bridgett decided to stop in and pay Kay a visit. She hadn't seen her since the day she'd met Adam. Besides, Bridgett could use some sage advice to help her get through Thanksgiving dinner tomorrow. She wondered if Kay ever tired of counseling the young people of Ramblewood. They'd all managed to turn to her for one reason or another through the years.

"I thought that was you driving Lexi's car." Kay held the side door open for Bridgett. "Come on in and I'll fix you a glass of sweet tea. By the look on your face, I don't think you came here for a purely social visit. Sit a spell and tell me what's on your mind."

"Tomorrow night we're having Thanksgiving at Clay's parents' house. All the families. Mine, Abby's, Clay's. It's a pre-wedding get together to introduce everyone. I'm excited to see Clay's sister because it's the first time Hannah's been home from college since August, but sitting down with Abby's family isn't exactly my idea of fun. And Clay went from being my friend to my future brother-in-law, which I never thought possible until recently. It's a whole lot of awkward. I don't even know what to call Abby's brother?"

"What's his name?" Kay asked.

"Wyatt."

"Call him Wyatt." Kay set a glass of sweet tea in front of Bridgett. "Stop overthinking this. You go there with the best of intentions and if you don't want to talk, just listen. You don't have to put on a show or impress anyone. Be yourself. Besides, out of all those people, only three of them are new to you. I'd venture to guess your mom will be more nervous than you are. And I'm sure she'd appreciate your support. While it might be uncomfortable, I promise you'll survive."

Bridgett sipped her tea. "What really gets me is that

I can't stop wondering what life would have been like if I'd been born first. I'll look at Abby's parents with the knowledge that they could've been my parents. That I might have grown up not knowing my real mother."

"True." Kay joined Bridgett at the table. "The empathy you have for Abby is commendable, but it happened to her. Not you. Playing the *what-if* game won't make it any easier. Do think for one minute that Abby hasn't run through the same scenario in her head. If she'd been born second, she would have had your life. Everything happens for a reason and we may not like it when does, but acceptance is a part of life."

"I think it's what comes after dinner that I'm most concerned about. Abby will once again ask me to go with her to visit Darren. She's spoken to him briefly, but she told me she feels as if she's betraying me by meeting him without me present. And I respect her position, but I never told her not to see him. She won't do it unless I tag along and I'm not sure I'm ready yet."

"Darren has a lot to think about this Thanksgiving, especially since his wife left. And who could blame her?" Kay swirled the long spoon in her glass. "I may not know Darren as well as my husband did, but when I heard he'd be alone on the holiday, I extended the invitation for him to come for Thanksgiving dinner. He turned it down, but the door's open if he changes his mind. I wouldn't want to offend you, Abby or your mother. It weighed heavily on my conscience whether or not to invite him, but in the end I chose to call. No one should be alone at Thanksgiving."

Kay's declaration surprised Bridgett. "Kay, this is

your house. I'm not upset because you invited Darren. But if he's not coming here, what is he doing for Thanksgiving?"

"He said he wanted to play golf during the day and planned to order room service for dinner."

"How sad." *No, this cannot be happening. I will not feel sorry for Darren.* "I'll bet his kids will call him or stop by." Bridgett still hadn't wrapped her head around the fact Darren's kids were her half siblings. For now, it was easier to think of them as his kids only.

"Maybe one or two will."

Bridgett understood Kay's double meaning instantly.

"You certainly don't make this easy, do you?" Bridgett asked.

Kay smiled over the top of her glass. "Finish your drink and find that man of yours."

"Okay, why don't you look happy?" Adam said as he met Bridgett on the walkway leading to the stables. "If you're having second thoughts about our plans, we can do it another day."

"It's nothing like that. Kay and I had a heart-to-heart talk about Thanksgiving dinner tomorrow. It's all good."

"If you're sure. Ready to head out?"

"Most definitely." Bridgett snaked her arms around Adam's neck, pulling him down for a kiss. "How far out is it?"

"See for yourself. Shane had to draw me a map. You can be the navigator." Adam held the truck door open for Bridgett. "Kay packed us a picnic dinner earlier.

When that woman makes fried chicken, she fries up enough to feed the state."

"It smells wonderful. She won't share that recipe, so savor every mouthful." Bridgett moved her handbag from the middle of the seat to the floor and slid closer to Adam. "I hope we don't wind up lost. A good portion of this ranch doesn't have cell service. I've always wondered why they haven't leased out a section for a cell tower."

"Probably because they want to maintain the aesthetics of the rolling hills."

They drove through Bridle Dance silently. Bridget's skin pricked each time Adam's arm bumped against hers. Her breath grew shallow in anticipation of the evening. Following the map, they drove down a narrow, tree-lined dirt road. What remained of the late afternoon sun filtered through the leaves of the thick canopy overhead, lending an almost magical quality to the road.

"I think Cooter Creek runs fairly close to here." Bridgett attempted to break the silence with small talk. They were alone, on a deserted road, with zero chance of anyone coming upon them. She'd come to a decision. Tonight she wanted to be with Adam. Bridgett smiled when she noticed the beads of sweat forming across his brow. He was as nervous as she was.

They pulled into a clearing next to Cooter Creek revealing a tiny silver Airstream trailer. Adam cut the truck's engine. He shifted slightly, the leather of his jacket creaking.

"I didn't bring you here to sleep with you, so I don't want you to feel pressured. I remember what you said about marriage before living together. We don't even have to go inside. We can build a fire and eat outside if you want."

The windows of the warm cab began to lightly fog. "That was about living together…I want to go in. I think this is the first time we've truly been alone, without the possibility of someone lurking nearby. Let's just see where it goes."

She hopped down from the truck, willing her feet to move. Nervousness rooted her to the dirt. Adam unlocked the trailer door and after he disappeared inside briefly, a warm glow lit the interior. Bridgett grabbed her bag from the truck and managed to cross the clearing without trembling…much. Stepping inside the Airstream, Bridgett immediately relaxed at the sight of cozy retrofitted furniture Lexi and Shane had installed.

"This is really cute." Bridgett sat on the edge of the couch. She watched Adam fumble with the cork on a bottle of red wine. Handing her a plastic glass, he removed the food Kay had packed. He fixed Bridgett a plate before joining her on the couch. "Thank you. Would it be terribly forward of me to admit I've thought about this moment since the day we met?"

Adam brushed her hair away from her shoulder, fully exposing her neck. The back of his fingers lightly grazed her skin sending a tingle of anticipation down to her core. "If nothing else, I'd be satisfied just holding you tonight."

"Now you're saying the words every woman longs to hear." Bridgett winked, tasting her food. "No man is every satisfied with cuddling."

Adam waved a chicken drum at her. "You're right. We would like a little nookie before the cuddling, but it's not a requirement. Heck, I'm happy with this."

"You sure about that?" Bridgett wiped her hands and set her plate next to her. She wound her fingers in his shirt, pulling herself up and across his lap until she straddled him. "Try to resist me," she whispered against his mouth.

Adam set his own plate aside. "I can't." He slid her jacket from her shoulders as their kiss deepened. He released her, and Bridgett stood, lifting her dress over her head. She turned her back to him, silently asking him to unclasp her bra. He groaned as she slid it from her arms, tossed it on the floor, and then faced him again. Satin ribbons held her turquoise blue panties in place. "May I?" Adam's eyes met hers, and then trailed down her body. He slowly tugged the ends, watching them slip from her hips.

"I've never seen anyone more beautiful in my life." Adam drew her to him, tasting each breast. Bridgett arched her back, allowing him full access to her body.

Adam rose before her, leading her to the bed. "Are you sure?"

Bridgett nodded. She hadn't been this certain of anything or anyone in all her life.

BRIDGETT AWOKE STILL wrapped in Adam's arms. Her body hummed from the past few hours. She chastised herself for any doubts she'd had about staying in Ramblewood. She'd not only given Adam her body, she'd given him her heart. He completed her.

The battery-operated bedside clock beamed 4:00 a.m. in the dimly lit trailer. Adam snored softly as Bridgett traced her fingers along a blue cobra tattoo covering his bicep. The artwork was stunning, but it seemed extremely out of character for Adam to have a snake with blood dripping from its fangs, as if it had just finished off a victim. She had noticed it earlier when he'd removed his shirt, but hadn't seen it clearly until now. She'd never had an opportunity to see his bare upper arms until tonight. It didn't matter, it was part of him and she loved every square inch. Bridgett shifted slightly and kissed his chest, trailing her way to his magnificently toned abs. Ranch work definitely did him good.

Adam's fingers ran through her hair. "What are you doing awake?"

Bridgett sought his mouth and kissed him. "I hate to break this up, but I have to be at The Magpie in an hour to start preparing for the charity lunch we're hosting today. And I need to stop by the Bed & Biscuit to shower and change first. Mazie's probably wondering where I've been all night."

"She's not wondering." Adam stretched. "Shane said if the Mustang was still at the ranch last night, Lexi would call Mazie and explain."

"The Lawson and Langtry families know we had sex. Wonderful." Bridgett pulled the pillow across her face.

"Only some of them." Adam lifted the sheet away, exposing her naked flesh to his view. "You've heard what they say about morning sex, right?"

"Supposedly it's the best there is." Bridgett rolled onto her back. "Care to see if we can top last night?"

"We don't have much time, but I'm willing to try."

Bridgett's eyes trailed down Adam's abdomen. "What are you waiting for? Let's put the theory to the test."

Adam definitely put to good use the short amount of time they had. Bridgett's legs shook like jelly as they walked to the truck. Bridgett fished in her bag for a rubber band, and loosely pulled her hair back into a ponytail. Bone-weary from their night together, Bridgett closed her eyes and rested her head against Adam's shoulder during their ride back. "I almost forgot, Happy Thanksgiving. Today I'm thankful for you." She opened her eyes and gazed up at him.

Adam kissed the top of her head. "I'm thankful for the greatest gift I ever could've received. The gift of a future with the woman I love. I never thought it was possible."

Love? Okay, it wasn't an outright *I love you*, but she'd take it.

Bridgett had detected a hint of sadness in his voice, and she wondered how badly he'd been hurt in the past. Not that the past mattered anymore. They had a future with one another and Bridgett finally allowed herself to believe in happily-ever-after.

Chapter Ten

After Adam dropped Bridgett off, he showered and met her back at The Magpie. He had offered to serve food for the Ramblewood Food Bank's annual Thanksgiving lunch for the less fortunate.

He tried to wrap his head around the decision he'd made while Bridgett was sleeping. Tonight, after Thanksgiving dinner with Abby and Clay's family, he would tell Bridgett the truth. He'd thought about telling her last night, but hadn't wanted to upset her right before she met Abby's parents and brother. He'd promised to stand beside her at dinner tonight, and he intended to keep that promise. At least that was the reason he gave himself for not coming clean when he had the perfect opportunity. He was scared to lose her and he never should have slept with her without full disclosure.

There was zero chance Bridgett would warmly welcome his revelation and Adam was fully prepared to leave Ramblewood—temporarily—if she asked him to. Once his identity became public knowledge, he'd have to leave his job at Bridle Dance and he did still need to head back to Los Angeles to handle a few financial matters in person.

Hopefully he'd be welcome in Ramblewood, but if he wasn't, one thing was for certain: LA was in his past. Spending a month and a half with Bridgett and the folks of Ramblewood had taught him how much he truly missed his Texas roots. He'd texted Lizzy earlier and told her he planned to tell Bridgett tonight and the rest of the world within a day or two.

"You're awfully pensive this morning." Bridgett wrapped her arms around Adam's waist from behind. "Still thinking about last night?"

Adam fought to hide the guilt and misery that threatened to shatter him. He looked down at Bridgett's hands clasped in front of him and attempted to commit the feeling of her body against his to memory—in case this was one of the last times they shared together. Turning into her embrace, Adam wrapped his arms around her. He studied Bridgett's face, wanting to remember her happy and content.

If Bridgett didn't forgive him, he would do whatever it took to win her heart again. They'd cemented their connection last night, and though she hadn't actually said so, Bridgett's love for him radiated off her. The words weren't necessary.

Adam's chest tightened. He dreaded tonight. He had all these new friends and a new life where people welcomed him into their homes and hearts, yet he couldn't completely do the same. He had become more of an imposter today than he'd been during his years in the band. The guilt gutted him. How deep could Bridgett's forgiveness possibly go? How much could she take before she didn't have any forgiveness left in her heart?

"Um, okay." Bridgett disengaged herself from his arms. "Did I misread us? I thought after last night we had moved forward but now I'm not so sure."

"What?" Adam shook his head and dragged himself to the present. "Bridgett, my feelings for you haven't lessened. They've definitely grown. I don't want to let you down."

"You won't. I have faith in—"

"Oh, my God!" Maggie shrieked from the kitchen. "Someone call 911."

Adam pulled his phone from his pocket and dialed as he and Bridgett ran into the kitchen. Maggie knelt before Bert, frantically wrapping towels around the bloodied hand he cradled.

"What happened?" Bridgett ran to Bert's side.

"The knife slipped." Bert swallowed hard. "It went into my palm and down into my wrist. I think I'm going to pass out."

"The ambulance is on the way." Adam moved the cooling racks out-of-the-way so the paramedics could freely enter the kitchen. "Hold his hand above his heart and put pressure on the cut."

Lark ran to the sink and wet some rags. Carrying them to Bert, she gently wiped his face in an attempt to calm him. Within seconds they heard sirens out front. They were lucky the ambulance corps was only two blocks away.

"Adam, can you unlock the front door and let them in?" Bridgett asked.

The paramedics quickly stabilized Bert and readied him for transport to the hospital, leaving the four of them staring down at the mess on the floor and the counter.

"What am I going to do?" Maggie ran her hands down her face. "I don't have a chef. And I should really go to the hospital with him."

"You have a chef. Me." Bridgett grabbed a mop and bucket from the storage room. "Maggie, go. I'll handle this. I'll just call the volunteers in a little early. We need to clean this mess up and sterilize everything. Are you okay to drive or do you want Lark to take you?"

"No, I'm okay." Maggie gave Bridgett a quick hug goodbye. "I'll call from the hospital."

Bridgett pulled on a pair of latex gloves. "Don't worry, I've got this covered."

Adam couldn't have been more impressed. An hour later, Bridgett had them back on schedule and a team of charity volunteers in place ahead of time, headed by none other than Abby. Bridgett took command of the kitchen and proved to be a solid leader. He didn't understand why Maggie hadn't used her in this capacity sooner.

"How are you holding up?" Adam whispered in Bridgett's ear as she peeled potatoes across from Abby who continued to chatter away about her upcoming wedding to anyone who'd listen. "Say the word and I'll trade you carrot duty."

Bridgett shook her head. "She actually does have good ideas. You should hear what she's planning to do to Slater's Mill on New Year's Eve. Somewhere in the midst of all of this I agreed to be her maid of honor."

"There's progress I hadn't expected." Adam playfully nudged Bridgett's arm. "Maybe you two will end up being the best of friends."

"Don't push your luck." Bridgett held up her potato peeler. "Baby steps here. Lord knows I'm trying."

"Well, I'm proud of you." Adam held his arms wide. "You have this place rockin' and rollin' in perfect rhythm." Adam inwardly winced at his choice of words.

"Interesting analogy." Bridgett tilted her head. "I guess I do. I love this sort of thing. I love to cook, and getting everyone together like this, especially when it it's for the food bank. Helping these families in need makes working on my day off worthwhile."

"This is your niche, Bridgett." Adam glanced around the kitchen. "You deserve your own restaurant, and if I have my way, one day you'll get it."

"THAT MAN HAS it bad for you," Abby said when Adam left the kitchen. "Clay told me you stayed the night in a travel trailer way out on the ranch."

"That didn't take long to get around." Bridgett groaned. Great, she'd given Ramblewood something new to talk about. "If you're looking for gossip, Abby, I don't kiss and tell."

"I don't want to hear about the kissing," Abby whispered. "Skip to the good stuff."

"I am not about to tell you what went on between the two of us last night."

"I seem to remember a certain someone asking me what I was doing out all night long a couple months ago." Abby pouted. "You said you wanted to live vicariously through me. Well, the shoe is on the other foot."

"That was different. You had a sex life and I didn't."

"Ah ha, so you did sleep with him last night. Way to go, sister." Abby high-fived Bridgett. "And for the record, when you asked me I had no sex life to speak of. Though one followed shortly afterward. If you can't talk to your sister about sex, who can you talk to?"

"It's real, isn't it?" Bridgett put down her potato peeler. "We truly are family."

"It's nice to see you accepting it," Abby said with a hint of satisfaction to her voice. "Maybe you'll let me in a little." Hurt shone in Abby's eyes—for once, she hadn't tried to hide it.

"Nothing about this has been easy, Abby. And I still don't have all the answers, but please understand, I never meant to hurt you."

"I know you didn't."

Abby kept her distance and didn't push Bridgett too far. She appreciated the gesture and understood where it came from, but she wanted to hug her sister. Though if she did, she'd turn into a blubbering mess and get the potatoes salty. "Truce?"

"Truce." Abby smiled and her eyes welled with tears. "I barreled into your town and turned your world upside down. I'm sorry, but I don't regret a single second of it. I'm glad you're my sister."

"Just don't expect me to call you my *big* sister, especially since you're a foot shorter than me."

"I am not a foot shorter. Half a foot maybe." Abby squared her shoulders and straightened her spine to gain as much height as she possibly could, then glanced at Bridgett. "Okay, maybe it's more like nine inches, but I am still older and you must respect your elders."

"You're older by thirty minutes. It doesn't count."

"And that's probably because your giraffe legs pushed me out. You only have yourself to blame for this."

Bridgett looked at Abby and the two women began laughing hysterically.

"You're probably right." Bridgett wiped her eyes. "I guess this year I should give thanks for you."

"You should give thanks for that hottie you've got going on over there in the corner." Bridgett followed Abby's eyes to Adam's backside. "When you get over yourself, you really need to tell me what happened last night."

"Hey, get your eyes off my man." Bridgett hip-checked Abby. "You have your wannabe Blake Shelton fiancé to drool over. You do kind of resemble Miranda Lambert. Although, I think she's taller than you."

"That's just not right. I sure wish I could sing like her."

"That night you and Clay kissed onstage in front of half the town, you two sure sounded like Blake and Miranda."

"First of all, he kissed me. And second, we were singing a duet between Kid Rock and Sheryl Crow."

"And that was the night we all knew you two were destined for one another." Bridgett wondered if anyone other than Abby looked at her and Adam thinking they were destined for one another, too. "I hope he means it when he says he doesn't plan on moving back to Katy."

"I get the impression he's here to stay." Abby said.

Bridgett shrugged. "But when he came to town he was embarking on a cross-country trip he never took."

Abby defiantly stared up at Bridgett. "Why don't you admit what really happened? As clichéd as it sounds, Adam had a falling out with his family and in the process of finding himself, he found you. He belongs here. He belongs with you. Accept it, Bridgett, and stop being so self-sabotaging."

Self-sabotaging? There was a phrase Bridgett hadn't associated with herself before. She wanted to deny the insult, but Abby was right. If anyone else had said those words to her, she would have come out fighting. Maybe she really needed to give this twin-sister thing a chance.

"How do you constantly stay positive?" Bridgett asked.

"When you've worked with the number of injured and disabled patients I have, you realize things could be much worse. I am grateful for everything I have. In a few hours, we'll feed so many people who couldn't afford to feed their families this Thanksgiving. People who can barely afford to feed their children on a daily basis. Compare their situation to ours and I can't see one reason not to have a positive outlook on life."

Well, that stung. Bridgett hadn't thought of herself as someone who wallowed in self-pity, but it was exactly what she'd done when she'd found out the truth about her family. Adam had done his best to say the same thing in a more delicate manner. But it had required Abby's take-no-prisoners attitude to jar her into reality.

Bridgett's family had grown to include a new sister and future brother-in-law. With them came a whole set of in-laws. She'd gone from her mom only to a very large family practically overnight.

Bridgett removed another turkey from the oven.

When she thought about Lexi's mixed family, Abby and Bridgett's situation wasn't that unique. Painful, yes, but Bridgett bet many twins had been separated at birth and never knew it.

Bridgett peeked through the kitchen pass-through at Adam who was mid-conversation with Abby's brother, Wyatt. Adam smiled and winked when he noticed her watching him. *Life happens.* And this was Bridgett's life, flaws and all. For the first time since she had discovered the truth about her parentage, Bridgett was okay with the situation. She was okay. Why had it taken her this long to realize she could survive a little bump in the road?

"It won't be today, but if you're still up for us sitting down with Darren together, I'm game. I can't promise how I'll react, but I will give him a chance to explain his side."

"Really?" Abby dropped her potato peeler and threw her arms around Bridgett's waist. "Thank you! You've made my day. First agreeing to be my maid of honor and now this."

Stunned by the smothering reaction she'd created, Bridgett began to laugh. Hugging her sister in return, Bridgett had to admit these moments with Abby had managed to make her smile. What was the old saying? If you can't beat them, join them. Bridgett had officially become a joiner.

ADAM HAD BEEN surprised when he'd walked into the kitchen and found Bridgett and Abby "hugging it out." They had finally resolved their differences.

Stepping outside, Adam dialed Lizzy.

"Happy Thanksgiving," Lizzy answered. "It's nice to actually hear from my brother on the holiday."

"Happy Thanksgiving, sis." Adam knew Lizzy was leery of his calls. "I'm not going to attempt to call Mom and Dad, but if you see them later please tell them I said Happy Thanksgiving, too. Did you get my text earlier?"

"I will and yes, I did. Good luck tonight." Skepticism was evident in Lizzy's voice. "I'll keep my phone on me in case you need me."

"Thank you. I'm sure I will." Adam didn't know if he should end the conversation or attempt normalcy with his sister. When he had called her in the past, it was either to tell her about himself or ask her to do something for him. "Are you spending the day with your boyfriend? What was his name again?"

"Allen. We're going to his parents' at noon and Mom and Dad's later tonight."

Adam smiled as he remembered the days of dating as a teenager and doing the double holiday meal. He'd never thought about doing it as an adult. Then again, the band had usually been on tour over the holidays.

"I hope you have fun. From what you've told me, Allen seems like a decent guy. I hope it works out for you."

"Thank you." He could hear the surprise in her voice.

"How are things in—what's the name of the town—Tumbleweed?"

"Ramblewood." Adam laughed. "I can see myself here for a long time."

"What about your place in LA?"

"It's sold. The closing is on Monday and I hired a

professional moving service to go in and box everything up for me. According to the manifest they emailed me, it's already on the way to Texas. I told you I was serious about leaving California for good."

"Do you really think they're going to accept you after you've lied all this time?"

"It's not the rest of the town I'm worried about. It's one person in particular."

"Just be realistic when you tell her. You've kept who you are from her for a month and a half, or close to it. When she finds out your reputation for being, well, an asshole—I hate to say it, but you were—how do you think she'll honestly react?"

Adam walked farther away from the building so no one would overhear him. "I've done nothing but been myself this entire time. The past ten years onstage I was pretending to be somebody else. The Snake doesn't exist. Adam Steele is real. I haven't lied to anyone, just the opposite. I've been more honest with people here and with myself than I have in years. Ramblewood and Bridgett have been great for me and I refuse to lose the woman I've grown to care about a great deal. She may be mad at me at first, but I'll do whatever it takes to prove myself to her."

"Don't you get tired of proving yourself and fixing your mistakes, Adam?" Lizzy countered. "That's exactly what you're doing with Mom and Dad. Trying to right a wrong. It's what you do. I'm sorry, but from where I stand it doesn't seem as if you've changed. You're continuing the same pattern in a different place, only you're calling it something else."

"That's not true."

"Sure it is," Lizzy argued. "If it wasn't, you would've told Bridgett who you were from day one. When you took the ranch job you could've told them who you are. Instead, you raced out and changed your driver's license. You weren't honest. Spin it however you want."

"You're not being fair."

"Who's talking about fair? I want you to see the cold hard facts before you get your hopes up. Prepare yourself, Adam. This isn't going to be easy."

"I know it won't." Adam knew Lizzy was right, but it didn't make the words any easier to take.

"I commend you for getting a job—because Lord knows you have enough money that you never have to work again—but what happened to the music school you wanted to build?"

"I still plan on it—"

"And I don't understand how working on this ranch is helping you earn any points with Mom and Dad. It's fine and wonderful, but it's been a month and it hasn't fixed anything. Stop talking about it and just do it already. Call me later and let me know how it went, good or bad. We haven't always had the best of relationships, but I love you and I'll always be there for you."

Adam swiped at the tears trailing down his cheeks. "I love you, too, Lizzy. I always have."

Adam hung up the phone and tried to compose himself before going back inside. He'd missed much of her adult life. And maybe if he'd been around, Lizzy wouldn't have gone through hell with her ex-husband.

Adam was determined to take care of Lizzy now,

despite her protests, but he knew it didn't make up for not being there when she'd needed him most. She had never once said anything to make him feel guilty for his absence. Maybe she didn't hold it against him. Still, he knew he needed to talk to her about it, and he would one day soon.

Today he would move forward and be thankful for what he had. Bridgett had become an unexpectedly huge part of his life and hopefully he'd find a way to repair the damage he'd do to their relationship tonight. And even if his family hated him, there was still a chance they could work things out.

"Adam," Bridgett called from the doorway. "Maggie's back. Are you all right?"

Adam turned around to face Bridgett. If he were smart, he'd tell her the truth right here and get it over with. But he wasn't going to do anything to detract from this Thanksgiving lunch.

"I'm good," Adam nodded. "I just had a talk with my sister and she basically kicked my butt."

Bridgett gave him the comforting hug. The rest of the world could wait for another minute or two. He just wanted to feel Bridgett's heart beating against his.

Chapter Eleven

"Thank you, everyone for another successful Thanksgiving charity lunch." Maggie stood behind the counter of The Magpie and addressed the room. "We wouldn't be able to do this every year without volunteers like you. Today I am thankful you all are a part of my life. God bless, and everyone go home to your families."

"Where would you like us to begin cleaning up?" Adam asked.

"I thought you and Bridgett were going to the Tanners' for dinner. Don't you two want to head over now?"

"There's no rush." Bridgett grabbed a box of industrial-strength garbage bags from under the counter. "And not for the reasons you might think. I am sure my mom is overwhelmed by the prospect of meeting Abby's adoptive parents, and it's probably better if I'm not there when it happens. She'll feel very self-conscious with me in the room."

"I heard you and Abby made peace today," Maggie said.

"Gee, I wonder what little songbird told you that."

Bridgett leaned past Maggie and waved to Lark. "Did she also tell you she has an interest in Abby's brother?"

"I do not," Lark said from across the room.

"It's funny how you picked up on that tidbit from so far away," Bridgett teased, recognizing the signs of a new crush. "Admit it, you've got it bad for the guy."

Lark flipped Bridgett the bird without another word, causing all of them to laugh.

"That's appropriate on Thanksgiving." Bridgett tucked her hands under her arms to form makeshift wings and strutted toward Lark. "Gobble, gobble."

Lark attempted to swat at her with a dishtowel and missed. "You know what they do to turkeys on Thanksgiving, don't you?"

Bridgett laughed. Only a little over a month ago she'd been quick to deny her own feelings for Adam. While their relationship had had its minor bumps, she wouldn't trade it for anything at this point. Adam had opened her eyes to what was right in front of her and she loved him for it. Well, for that and many other reasons. She couldn't help smiling when his eyes met hers.

Quickly looking away, Bridgett pried a bag from the box. "Let's clean up and head out of here. You know the offer still stands for you to join us at Clay's parents' house for dinner. They won't mind."

"Thank you, but I accepted Maggie's dinner invitation earlier," Lark said.

"It only took me asking her twenty times before she finally relented."

"I can't believe that after all the turkey we served

here today, you're going home to fix dinner," Adam said. "You are a glutton for punishment."

"I'm not cooking," Maggie wiped down one of the tables. "My husband is. Thanksgiving dinner is his contribution to the holiday. He insists on doing it every year, even if it's only the two of us and Bert. This year my daughter and her family are coming over."

"It's too bad Bert wasn't able to see all of this come to fruition today," Bridgett looked around the luncheonette. "He loves this and the Mistletoe Rodeo charity dinner."

"Did that man ever give me a battle about dropping him off at our house after the hospital. He was determined to come back here to his kitchen. But those doctors had him so doped up on painkillers I was afraid he'd fall in the gravy and drown. He's in much safer hands with my husband."

"He's lucky he didn't sever a tendon or an artery," Adam said. "You'll have your hands full without him for a while."

"We'll be okay," Maggie said. "I'll man the grill, Bridgett will take over the baking and Lark will wait tables. We managed for a long time with only one waitress—we'll be fine until Bert is able to come back to work."

Bridgett appreciated Maggie's faith in her. Filling her boss's shoes wouldn't be easy, but she was up for the challenge. Bridgett slid under Adam's arm and tucked herself next to him, enjoying the warmth of his body beside her. She might be nervous to meet Abby's family this evening, but Adam gave her the strength she needed to plow through it. She couldn't imagine a better man to have by her side.

FOR THE NEXT HOUR, they worked together scrubbing the restaurant from top to bottom until no sign of today's luncheon remained. Adam heard a couple of the volunteers out behind the kitchen, singing and playing guitar. His fingers still itched to play every day, and luckily, he was able to use one of the old timer's guitars at the ranch. Confident the man had no idea who he was, Adam had allowed himself the pleasure of playing for him.

In a couple of hours he wouldn't have to hide his identity any longer. Confident no one would suddenly recognize him, Adam decided to join them. Borrowing a guitar, he led everyone in an acoustic rendition of "We Can Work it Out" by the Beatles.

The fret board beneath his fingers was pure heaven, not as good as being with Bridgett, but damn close. The guitar he played was nowhere near as expensive as his one-of-a-kind custom Guild acoustic, but it didn't need to be. He was making music, and that had always been his first love.

Owning a music school ranked pretty high on his list, and now that Bridgett was in the picture, she had trumped them all. The chance of making his dreams come true was at his fingertips, and after tonight there was nothing stopping him from opening his school in town and playing the kind of music he enjoyed…unless Bridgett decided not to forgive him.

"I knew it." Lark stood in the doorway glaring

at Adam. "I knew I'd seen you somewhere before. I couldn't place where, but I knew your voice."

Everyone stopped singing and stared at Adam.

Bridgett stepped outside. "Lark, what's going on?"

"It's him." Lark's voice was thick with disgust. "I have to hand it to you, you clean up good."

"I don't understand." Bridgett's eyes blinked rapidly.

Adam stood, handing the guitar to one of the guys. "I planned to tell you tonight. Somewhere private." His heart pounded in his ears, almost deafening him. "My name is Adam Steele, but for the past ten years, people have known me as The Snake." There, he'd said it. It was out. He'd told her the truth. Adam inhaled sharply, waiting for her to respond.

"No." Bridgett shook her head. "No, I don't believe you."

"I practically didn't recognize you," Lark chided. "Your singing gave you away, though. Very reminiscent of one of your earlier ballads, before you became so angry."

"Adam?" Bridgett questioned. "I've seen The Snake and you look nothing like him."

"Change the hair, give him a beard and it's him. Bridgett, he's lied to you all this time." Lark whipped her phone from her pocket. "Here, I'll show you."

Bridgett held Lark's phone as a video of Adam's band played. She looked from the phone to Adam and back again, and Adam knew she was trying to accept what she was seeing.

"This is really you." Tears fell silently from Bridgett's eyes. "But I heard on the radio you were in Australia."

"That was my body double." The words sounded ridiculous to him. "We sent him there to keep people from discovering the truth. I wanted to give you and my family a heads-up first. This should have occurred in several methodical stages. There are press releases and—it doesn't matter anymore."

"I was part of a methodical stage?" Color drained from Bridgett's face, causing Adam to regret his poor choice of phrasing. "How could you do this to me? Do you have any idea what it feels like to be betrayed and humiliated in front of an entire town…twice?"

"It gets better. Have you seen him with Miss July?" Lark chided, showing Bridgett more photos.

"Really, Lark?" Adam tried to lunge for the phone, but she snatched it away from his grasp. "You could have made your point without showing her those." He hadn't wanted Bridgett to see him in bed with another woman. She deserved better. He had been a fool for thinking she'd forgive him after this.

"You're serious?" Lark squared her shoulders. "Bridgett deserves to hear the truth. You lied to her. To all of us."

"Those photos are only hurting her more," Adam growled. "You are no friend if you drive the knife deeper. I take full responsibility for what I did, but Lark there is no need to be cruel to Bridgett."

Bridgett brought the photo closer to her face and studied it. A visible chill shuddered through her body. She handed the phone back to Lark. "Give us privacy please," Bridgett said, her voice low and quiet. "Lark, that means you, too."

"I'll be right inside. You yell if you need me."

Bridgett nodded and waited for the door to close. "This is why your parents disowned you. Because you told the whole world you didn't have parents. Your rags-to-riches story was bullshit." Bridgett glared at him, her eyes devoid of any emotion. "People looked up to you. I promise you, I was never one of them. But kids worshipped you. They thought if you could make it maybe they could, too. But you're nothing but a fake. Why did you do this? Why string me along with a lie?"

"It's complicated," Adam began. "At first I didn't want to risk blowing my cover."

"Your cover?" Bridgett stepped away from him. "This was a cover? You slept with me and spewed all this crap about a future together. So what was real and what wasn't?"

"I meant every word of it." This was not going as Adam had planned. "I knew I had to tell you the truth. I wanted to from the beginning. But when you mentioned all the lies your mother had told you I was afraid. I thought if I told you everything, I would have never had a chance to get to know you."

"You should've learned from my mother's mistakes that keeping secrets only damages a relationship. I don't know if I will ever get back to where I was with my mother and that breaks my heart every day. And knowing what I'd already been through, you went and did the same thing. I don't even know who you are. I trusted you. I confided in you things I hadn't told anyone else."

"I didn't want to lose you."

The pain in her eyes was a sight he had feared since

day one. "It's too late. I'm gone, Adam. You committed the ultimate sin in my book. You lied. It's not about who you are or who you aren't. Yeah, that's major— huge! But it's not about that. You lied to me. You had a front-row seat to not only my reaction to what my mother and Darren did, but deepest feelings about it. You took advantage." Bridgett turned away from him. "You kn— I can't—I can't do this."

"Bridgett, don't believe everything you read and those tabloids," Adam pleaded. Watching her walk away tore his heart in two. "You are the first person I've told the entire truth to. Miami was a lie—a lie my first manager made up in order to sell records. It was a lie I was stuck with and one I fought to correct over the years. My management company said it would damage our reputation, so I just went with it. I allowed other people to control my life and I've regretted it since."

Bridgett spun to face him. "Is your sister really in Texas?"

"Yes, Lizzy lives in Katy. So do my parents. They have their own ranch, and my sister lives in a house I bought for her to live in after her husband beat her up."

"You told me your sister's hands were damaged from her ex, you didn't tell me you bought her a house to live in. You left quite a bit out, Adam."

Thankful Bridgett hadn't walked away, Adam attempted to explain his lies and omissions. "I bought her a house in a security-patrolled development. You can easily look at the register of deeds online and you will see it in my name…Adam Steele. I sold my house in Los Angeles after I met you. The closing is on Monday. Everything I owned is already on its way to a storage facility here in Texas. I have no intention of going back to California except to wrap up a few more business items. I'll only be there for a day or two. Ramblewood is my home now."

Bridgett recoiled from Adam's touch when he tried in vain to reach for her.

"Don't," she warned.

"Bridgett," Adam said softly. "Ask me anything, but don't run away from me. Please don't shut me out. I'll answer any of your questions but please don't leave me."

Bridgett shook her head and just stood there without saying a word. He was grateful she was at least listening to him.

"You had so many opportunities to tell me the truth," Bridgett said without making eye contact.

"It broke my heart not to tell you the truth." Adam wasn't going to deny or even attempt to justify why he'd kept the truth from her. "When I came to Ramblewood, I was driving from Katy to Los Angeles. I had just come off a bad tour—the band had collectively decided to break up the night before and I'd ended up at my parents' house. They slammed the door in my face and I couldn't blame them. I turned to my sister for help and she cleaned me up. When she finished, I didn't even recognize myself. We tested it by running to the store to get some more appropriate clothing, and when nobody recognized me I decided to drive home to Los Angeles to regroup. It was the first time I was able to be in public without fans or paparazzi mobbing me. If

I had let everyone in Ramblewood know who I was, I wouldn't have had the chance to start over."

"Were you really going to make all those tourist attraction stops you told me about or was that another lie?" Bridgett asked, finally meeting his eyes.

"All of that was true." Adam's hands shook. He jammed them in his jeans pockets to prevent himself from reaching for her again.

"It doesn't make any sense." Bridgett folded her arms across her chest.

"What doesn't?"

"You working at the ranch. You clearly didn't need the money, so why put yourself through the hard work every day?"

"For exactly that reason—it *was* hard work and I craved it. I needed to feel useful. I wanted to wake up with a purpose every day. Standing onstage in front of thousands of people is not as wonderful as you might think. Once the fans leave and you're back on that tour bus, you have nothing. The adrenaline only flows when you're onstage, and unless you have something or someone else to go home to, it's a very lonely place to be. My bandmates have wives and families, I don't. I'd never loved anyone until I met you. I never saw myself settling down, getting married or falling in love. I never thought I deserved it. But my opinion has changed because of you."

"My opinion has changed, too. I don't know how to love someone who has lied to me from day one. You let me down. I mean *really* let me down, Adam." Tears streamed down Bridgett's cheeks. "You changed my whole outlook on life and now I feel more cheated than I did before you came to town."

"Would you have given me the time of day if you knew the truth from the very beginning?"

Bridgett swiped at her cheeks with her fingertips. "Probably not. At least not at first. But if you stuck around long enough maybe I would have."

"I wanted a chance with you so desperately, and I took the biggest risk of my life. Maybe I was wrong, but I wouldn't trade one minute we spent together for anything. I would gladly give everything away and work on a ranch for the rest of my life if it meant I could be with you."

"I have to go. I have a family dinner to get through and I'll need to explain your absence. Please don't show up."

"I won't."

Adam's heart broke into a million pieces as Bridgett turned and walked through the door of the luncheonette. Lark stepped outside again, and for a moment he thought she'd tell him off one more time. Instead, she studied him silently for a few long minutes and then followed Bridgett inside. Adam didn't know her background; no one did, but he suspected it wasn't a very pretty one. Maybe she understood more than she let on.

By now, the Langtrys had probably already heard part of the story, considering Maggie's daughter was married to one of them. He needed to make his apologies and clear out of their place tonight, if they hadn't already bundled his stuff and left it on the main road. Climbing into his truck, Adam scrolled through his phone for local hotel listings. He wasn't giving up on Bridgett so easily. He'd fix this. He had to.

Adam turned the key in the ignition, and rested his head against the steering wheel. The wetness on his own cheeks took him by surprise. His chest heaved, his heart aching at the thought of never seeing Bridgett again.

"AM I A FOOL for believing him?" Bridgett asked.

Lark shook her head. "No, I don't think so. I hate to admit it, but much of what he said made sense. And yes, I listened at the door. None of us would've given him a chance if we knew who he really was. And he's right, you can't believe everything you read online. What was he like when you were together?"

"He was like a normal guy." Bridgett flashed through their nights out. "I guess that's what he wanted. No fans, no photographs." She inwardly laughed. "The day we met, I asked if he was a reporter. He told me he'd been called plenty of things, but never that. It makes sense. He hated reporters as much as I did. I keep replaying conversations in my head. I can see where he almost told me the truth many times. He was on the verge. And half the time, I cut him short because I thought he was referring to my situation. I guess I need to learn it's not all about me."

Lark gave Bridgett a hug. "Are you going to be okay?"

"I've been worse." Bridgett laughed. "If I can get through the twin debacle and tonight's dinner, I think I can survive this."

Bridgett held up her hand for a high-five, and Lark met it.

"You're a strong woman, Bridgett."

"Hell, I just want to toss back a bourbon or two." Bridgett laughed. "Let me go get changed and head over to the Tanners' for family fun night. I think I owe a few people an apology of my own."

She knew dinner would be difficult, but she'd promised her mom they'd celebrate the holiday together. Enough promises had been broken for one night and too many people had been hurt lately. She'd let her heart finish breaking over Adam in a few hours. Right now, her mother, Abby and she needed to heal as a family.

Chapter Twelve

Adam sat in the truck for a long time before he built up the nerve to drive on to the Bridle Dance Ranch. Then, stealing his nerves, he climbed Kay Langtry's front-porch stairs. He no longer felt comfortable using the side or the back entrances reserved for friends and family.

Kay was probably about to sit down to Thanksgiving dinner with her family, but he wanted her and the rest of the Langtrys to hear the truth from him. The door opened and Kay invited him in, leading him toward the dining room where everyone sat around a turkey ready to be carved.

"We've been expecting you," Shane said.

"I bet." Adam nervously jammed his hands into his jeans pockets. "I'll make this short so you can get back to your dinner. You've probably heard the majority of it already anyway."

"Maggie called and said you had something important to tell us," Kay said. "But she said we needed to hear it directly from you."

Thank God for small miracles.

"When I came to Ramblewood, I was on a mission

of sorts to find myself. I am known worldwide by the name The Snake, and I am the lead singer of a rock band known for leaving a mass of destruction in its wake. When I first came on the music scene, my ex-manager created a fake biography that said I was a street performer from Miami with no family to call my own. He felt it would sell more records than the truth—that I'm a small-town Texas boy. Over the years that persona morphed into someone who was known more for his offstage antics than his onstage performance."

"Was anything you told us true?" Lexi asked.

"All of it was. It was what I purposely left out that matters now. When I stopped in Ramblewood to check out your Harvest Festival, I had only intended on staying for the weekend. It's no secret I fell in love with Bridgett, but I also fell in love with the community. I wanted to get back to my roots. I never lied to Bridgett or any of you. I haven't been so open and honest with people in my life, and it was amazingly freeing. I wanted—needed—to feel human again and that's why I asked you for a job."

"You probably have more money than we do," Shane grumbled.

"My net worth has been publicized repeatedly. It's not hard to find on the internet so I will let you be the judge of that one. I wanted you to hear the truth from me, since it came out today after the charity lunch. I'm truly sorry for deceiving you."

"And Bridgett?" Lexi asked.

"I've told Bridgett the entire truth. I'm afraid I may have destroyed my relationship with her for good and—

and I'm having a hard time accepting it. I need you to know my feelings for her are sincere and everything I've done and said has been real. But I am guilty by omission, and I don't deserve your forgiveness so I won't ask for it."

"You're the one who sent in that large anonymous donation to Dance of Hope the first week you were here," Kay said. "I remember how moved you were by our hippotherapy program and the donation arrived the following day. I had my suspicions then that it was you."

"But you didn't say anything." Adam was surprised to hear that from day one Kay had questioned his story. "Why didn't you ask me?"

"People send donations anonymously for a reason and I respected your privacy. Besides, I wasn't certain it was you."

"Mom's not the only one who thought there might be more to your story," Shane added. "After you filled out your employment paperwork, Kenny left it on my desk for me to determine if we needed to do a background check. Certain positions require verification. Ranch hands typically don't, so I decided not to do the check. But I did question why your temporary driver's license had been issued two days before you started working for us. I wondered if you'd really lost yours or if there was more to it. I gave you the benefit of the doubt, even though I had the opportunity to find out for sure. We have had plenty of people on this ranch come here for a second chance at life. You wouldn't be the first and as long as you were genuine and honest with us from the beginning, I decided to overlook it."

"You knew he wasn't legit?" Lexi was surprised to

hear her husband kept a secret from her. "He dated my best friend. Didn't you think you owed it to Bridgett to check him out?"

Shane rubbed his forehead. "Heavens knows I'm going to regret this, but Lexi, we've all made mistakes, you and me included. This was between Bridgett and Adam."

"No one is perfect." Kay's authoritative voice rose above the side chatter. "None of us at this table have the right to judge you or anyone else. You're correct about not having to ask for our forgiveness, because there's nothing to forgive. What happened before you came to Ramblewood was in your past. You're telling us you've been honest since the time you arrived and I for one believe you."

"So do I." Shane stood.

One by one the entire family rose. Lexi stood last, which Adam understood in view of her relationship with Bridgett.

"I'm at a loss here. Thank you."

Kay waved for everyone to slide down one seat and pulled out a chair for Adam. "Now, let's eat before the rest of this food gets cold."

Adam took his place at the table and watched the entire Langtry family continue to chat and pass the serving dishes as if the entire conversation had never happened. He only wished he could have this kind of relationship with his own family. Tonight he needed them more than ever.

BRIDGETT WAS ABLE to get in and out of the Bed & Biscuit without any questions from Mazie. News hadn't traveled that far yet and Bridgett knew she only had a matter of minutes to shower and change before Mazie found out.

Pulling up in front of Clay's parents' house, Bridgett vowed not to let what had happened with Adam ruin everyone else's Thanksgiving. Inhaling deeply, she pushed her shoulders back and strutted up the front walk as if she walked a fashion runway. *I can do this.*

Abby swung the door open before Bridgett had a chance to knock.

"Bridgett, you look amazing. I love your dress. Where's Adam?"

"He couldn't make it." Bridgett didn't offer any further explanation, but she was certain Abby sensed she wasn't telling her the whole story. She didn't push for more information and Bridgett didn't offer. By the end of the night, the entire town would hear about her humiliation once again. For a few short hours, she wanted to forget she'd ever heard the name Adam Steele.

"Come meet my parents."

Bridgett had thought she'd be nervous meeting Abby's parents, but she hadn't taken into account how they would feel. It must be hard for them meeting Abby's biological family, especially since their daughter had given up her entire life and moved to Texas to be closer to them. Her adoptive parents appeared painfully awkward and out of place despite Abby's constant physical reassurance of a hand touch here and a hug there.

And Bridgett's poor mother...she had never seen Ruby so quiet unless she was sleeping. Knowing her mother, she was mentally comparing herself to Abby's parents. Seeing how much wealthier they were than Ruby, Bridgett knew her mother once again felt as if she had failed her. It broke Bridgett's heart.

Dinner went relatively well. Bridgett was grateful Hannah was home from college. Hearing about college sororities and exams over turkey and pumpkin pie was a fun distraction from her own thoughts and feelings. Slipping out the back after dinner, Bridgett sat on one of the porch's wooden rocking chairs and enjoyed the cool night air and solitude.

"Mind if I join you?" Abby asked.

"Be my guest." Bridgett pointed to the other chair. "I wasn't trying to be rude. I just needed some fresh air. It's been a very long day."

"You and me both," Abby agreed. "Be glad you're outside. My brother just told my parents he wants to move here. They're not happy. The only reason he moved to Charleston in the first place was because I was there and the city had a decent university for him to attend. It doesn't make sense for him to stay there now that he's graduating. Plus he can't afford the expenses on the house we shared. And after living in the south for four years, he doesn't want to return to Pennsylvania's frigid winters. He's always wanted to be a police officer or a private investigator. Now that Wyatt will have his criminal justice degree, Clay's been talking to him about his options, including working for him at the detective agency. Ramblewood does make sense. But it's his decision, not theirs."

"Abby, I don't think that's why they have a problem with it." As intuitive as Abby was, Bridgett was surprised she hadn't realized why her parents were opposed to her brother's move. "Look at it from their point of view. They adopted you, gave you a home and raised you as if you were their own. Then you tracked down your long-lost sister and moved here to be near your biological parents and me. Then your brother follows. Your parents probably feel left out and possibly even cut out of your lives. I'm willing to bet they already feel as if you're replacing them with your new family."

"That's not at all what I'm doing."

Bridgett leaned over and squeezed Abby's hand. "I know you're not, although I can't help but feel like you're invading my territory, and I need to work on that. Wyatt needs to be a little more sympathetic to the situation. I'm not saying he shouldn't move here, but he needs to be aware of how his actions are affecting your mom and dad. Because at the end of the day, despite all of this biological crap, they are still your parents."

"You're right."

Abby sat in silence for the next few minutes. Bridgett felt her eyelids getting heavier with every rock of her chair. The L-tryptophan from the turkey didn't help matters much. After the little sleep she'd had last night—no—she refused to spend one second remembering her night with Adam after what he'd told her today.

"If you want to talk about it, I can be a good listener—contrary to popular belief."

Bridgett let out a long breath. "I don't know if you would believe me if I told you."

"Try me."

Bridgett opened her eyes and regarded Abby for who she was, her sister. If you can't trust your sister, who can you trust?

By the time Bridgett finished with her story, Abby's mouth gaped open in shock.

"There's only one surefire way to find out the truth," Abby finally said when she regained the use of her vocal chords. "We'll have Clay run a full background check on him. You deserve to get all the facts and find out if his whole explanation is true."

As much as Bridgett hated to involve Clay and Abby, she did want the truth…and whatever harsh realities came with it.

ADAM HADN'T FELT comfortable sleeping in the bunkhouse last night, or accepting Kay's invitation to stay in the main house. He opted to spend the night in a hotel, and booked a round-trip flight to Los Angeles so he could sign off on whatever paperwork remained to sever all ties with his old life.

Shane had agreed to keep Adam's truck at the ranch until he returned. By the time he made it down to the hotel lobby, airport car service was waiting. As they drove out of town, Adam realized he was carrying more baggage than he'd arrived with. He'd be flying home to California with a broken heart.

TAKING A BREAK from her shift at The Magpie the next day, Bridgett ducked outside to call Lexi and find out what had happened when Adam arrived last night.

"He explained what he did and joined us for dinner," Lexi said matter-of-factly.

"Awfully bold of him, don't you think." Adam definitely wasn't the man she'd thought he was. She hadn't imagined he'd be that brazen after revealing he had lied to her for almost two months.

"It didn't quite happen the way you think. Everyone asked him to stay."

"Including you?" Lexi's betrayal pierced what was left of Bridgett's heart, almost causing her to hang up the phone. "How could you?" she whispered.

"It wasn't easy," Lexi said. "How do I explain it?" She exhaled into the phone. "I believe him. I know it's not what you want to hear, but I don't think he lied to you. He did leave out some very crucial details and you have every right to be mad at him for that."

Bridgett couldn't fathom what she was hearing. "Let me guess, he's working as a ranch hand and everything is wonderful in Adam's world."

"Um, no. I thought he would have told you," Lexi said. "He left for California this morning. He's gone, Bridgett."

Bridgett's stomach churned and her heart began to thud a slow, heavy beat. "He told me Ramblewood was his home now."

"If it's any consolation, Shane has his truck and Adam claims he's going to be back, although we do have our doubts about it. There's no comparison between LA and Ramblewood. I'm sorry, sweetie. I shouldn't have said that. Do you even know if you still want him around?"

"I don't know. He told me everything was finished in California…that he'd sold his house and had already shipped his furniture to some warehouse. But I don't know if there's more he's not saying, either."

"First I've heard about any of that stuff, but I would think the dissolution of a platinum-selling band would require signing mountains of paperwork. Have you checked out his net worth? Bridgett, there's a lot of money at stake and I'm not sure how much of it could be handled long-distance."

"He did say he had to go back to wrap things up. How much of its true is anyone's guess." Bridgett ended the conversation with Lexi feeling worse than she had before. She had tried calling Adam, but it had gone straight to voice mail. Not bothering to leave a message, she disconnected.

After work, Bridgett decided to drive out to Bridle Dance and talk to Kay personally. If Adam had confided in anyone, she suspected it would have been Kay.

"You're okay with Adam's lies, too?" Bridgett asked Kay as they walked along the main ranch road.

"I know you're hurting and I can only imagine how betrayed you must feel. But from what I can reckon, the man told the truth the entire time he was here." Kay stilled Bridgett from walking farther. "When it really comes down to it, what lies did he tell you, or any of us? He's a horseman from Katy, Texas, who had a bad falling out with his family. He's a cowboy who lost his way. Not unlike any of my boys at some point in their lives. Yes, he did it with much more dramatic flair than any of them, but it still doesn't change the facts, Bridgett. Adam told us the truth from day one. It's the rest of the world he lied to. I know this is a lot to ask, but I think he deserves a second chance."

"He lied by omission."

"Who hasn't?" Kay threw back her head and laughed. "Don't even begin to tell me you haven't done the exact same things. We all do. We purposely leave something out because it might hurt someone or because we're afraid of losing their love or respect. Does Ruby have any idea you used to sneak out here for riding lessons?"

Bridgett shook her head. "No."

"Why not? Why keep it from her?" Kay goaded.

"Because she would have felt like a charity case if she'd found out Joe wasn't charging me for the lessons."

"And what about all those crazy things you used to do when it came to boys? Does Adam know about the time you fell and broke your arm because you had such a crush on Aaron Bradley you chased him up a tree? No, because it's not who you are today. Adam left things out because it's not who he is today. And yes, hiding his identity was much bigger than falling out of a tree, but Adam was trying to move forward with his life. Nothing he hid was threatening or physically harmful to anyone. I know you were hurt by it, and you have a right to be upset. But it isn't always black and white. You have to allow for gray, too. He's a good man, Bridgett. I shouldn't tell you this, but he made a large anonymous donation to Dance of Hope the first few days he was here."

"He did what?"

"I'm not going to give you the amount," Kay smiled. "But he added lots of zeros to the check."

Bridgett thanked Kay and sought out her sister at Dance of Hope. She needed Clay to locate Adam for her so she could talk to the man who'd come to mean so much to her before he'd broken her heart. If it meant flying to California, she'd be on the next plane out. She refused to let things end this way.

Chapter Thirteen

Days passed and Bridgett was no closer to finding Adam. Where the stares and whispers had once begun to wane, they were now in full swing again. She'd moved home with her mother after Thanksgiving, and while it was a start, they still had a long ways to go before they repaired their relationship.

Clay had run a detailed background check on Adam. It turned out everything he'd told them was true. By the week's end, Adam's face was plastered across every trashy tabloid at the grocery store checkout. He had done exactly what he'd said he would. He'd told the world the truth. While he had refused interviews, Bridgett had read every one of his press releases.

Despite Clay's various connections in Los Angeles, Adam had the money to hide and stay hidden. For all she knew, he might actually be trekking the Australian outback this time. It was the last place anyone would check now.

She had been able to contact Adam's sister, Lizzy. Clay had located her phone number and Bridgett had listened while his sister told her the extent of Adam's deception. Lizzy loved her brother, but she hadn't sugar-coated any of it. She gave Bridgett the facts and told her to come to her own conclusions. Bridgett just wanted Adam to return one phone call. That was all she needed.

ADAM LANDED AT the San Antonio airport exactly two weeks after he'd left. With all ties severed in California, he finally felt free. During his time away, he had researched every available property in Ramblewood.

Eager to fulfill one of his lifelong dreams, he found a storefront for his music school. He also found a large house near the center of town on a few acres with a commercially zoned separate building he'd love to convert into a restaurant for Bridgett, if she'd have him back. She had at least left him a few voice mails, asking him to call her back. It had given him a glimmer of hope, but he hadn't felt right returning her calls yet. He'd wanted to ensure he'd wrapped up everything before he spoke with her again.

Adam had an appointment to meet with Bond Gallo, a Ramblewood real estate agent, in a little over an hour. If the properties he'd looked at online were as good in person, Bond would have one hell of a commission check this month.

As much as he wanted to see Bridgett, there were a few minor details he needed to tie up first. He knew Bridgett would never want to be the wife of a rock star, but the wife of a music school owner was altogether different.

When airport car service pulled up to the first property, Adam was pleasantly surprised.

The main house was magnificent, needing very little updating. The old farmhouse that stood on the property was the perfect size for a restaurant and he'd be willing to pay for whatever modifications Bridgett wanted. It needed to be completely gutted and outfitted for an industrial kitchen, but he was confident it would maintain much of its charm.

"It's perfect," Adam said to Bond.

The commercial property Bond had shown Adam for his music school had far exceeded his expectations in size. It was an abandoned ammunitions factory. The inside was a blank slate and could be configured any way he wanted. Adam made two full price offers that afternoon, setting his final plan in motion.

Adam asked his driver to take him to the back entrance of the Bridle Dance ranch, closest to Shane and Lexi's house. He wasn't ready for anyone to spot him just yet. He wanted to be the one to tell Bridgett he was back in town.

Adam dialed Shane's number and was grateful Shane didn't give away who he was talking to when he answered the phone.

"How are you doing?" Shane asked.

"You're about to find out, because I'm almost to the ranch. Is there any way you can get me my truck without anyone seeing you?"

"Come on up to the house. Lexi's not home."

By nightfall, with Shane's seal of approval, Adam headed toward Ruby's house to see Bridgett. He was surprised to hear she'd moved back home. He wondered what had changed her mind, but was glad she had finally resolved her family differences. Unfortunately, he couldn't quite say the same for himself. Things still hadn't improved with his parents, although his relationship with Lizzy was growing stronger every time they spoke.

Adam's Texas cell phone rang and he was surprised to see Bridgett's name and photo on the screen. He wondered if Shane had told Lexi and she had tipped Bridgett off that he was in town. It didn't matter anyway: he was almost to her house.

"Hello."

"I wasn't sure if you'd answer." Bridgett said on the other end. "Hear me out before you hang up on me."

"I have no intention on hanging up on you, Bridgett."

"That's good because I have a lot to say."

"Can it wait a minute?" Adam asked.

"No, it can't. I've waited two weeks for you to pick up the phone. I've done a lot of soul-searching and I know in my heart you are the man I want to spend the rest of my life with. You said you wanted a second chance, and I'm ready to give you one, even if it means going to California."

Adam heard the words, but his brain had a hard time keeping up with her. "Are you sure, because if you are, I have something to ask you first."

"Okay." Adam could hear the anxiety in Bridgett's voice. He had debated telling her about his plans in person, but he didn't think he'd be able to endure the rejection if she were standing in front of him.

"How would you feel if I bought a house in Ramblewood and opened up a music school nearby?"

"A music school?"

Adam pulled up in front of Bridgett's house and parked. "I wanted to tell you the night you asked me what my hopes and dreams were. But I couldn't. Not then, I couldn't. It had been my plan from the beginning. I've designed and redesigned it many times over the years and I'm ready."

"Is that what you really want?" Bridgett asked. "To leave Hollywood and the standard of living you've grown so accustomed to."

He opened the truck door and stepped onto the sidewalk. "I've never been happy or comfortable in California. Don't get me wrong—it's a beautiful place, but it can also be very ugly at times. I got caught up in that lifestyle years ago." Standing outside her front door, Adam inhaled deeply. "I know I still have a lot of work to do when it comes to my family, but I love you, Bridgett. With you by my side, I know I can accomplish anything."

"I love you, too, Adam."

Adam heard the doorbell through Bridgett's end of the phone.

"Answer the door, Bridgett."

"Of all times for someone to show up at the house." Adam tried not to laugh at Bridgett's frustration. "Hold on a second."

The front door to the house swung open, fast and furious.

"Oh, my God." Bridgett dropped the phone. "You're here."

Adam knelt on one knee before Bridgett and held a ring box out in front of him.

"Bridgett Jameson…" Adam slowly opened the box, revealing a two-carat pear-shaped diamond set in a delicate diamond accented white-gold band. He knew she'd balk at anything larger. "Will you do me the honor of becoming my wife?"

Bridgett's hands flew to her chest. "I—I don't know what to say."

"*Yes* is customary, that is, if you'll have me."

"Yes!"

Adam pulled away and removed the ring from the box. Lifting her hand he slid it onto Bridgett's finger.

"I've secretly envisioned this moment from the day we met," Adam said. "I can't wait to make you my wife."

"How does *soon* sound?"

Epilogue

Bridgett and Adam accepted Abby and Clay's generous offer to join them in a double New Year's Eve wedding ceremony at Slater's Mill. Abby spared no detail in decorating the honky-tonk to look like a sparkling country fantasyland. Since it had been Abby's wedding to begin with, Bridgett went along with whatever she chose and didn't try to change a single thing. Bridgett had never imagined a place so rustic would look so romantic. The decorations even lined the back deck and all along Cooter Creek. It was perfect in every way possible. Abby and Clay had wanted to marry in the place where they shared their first kiss.

They'd sent silver-engraved invitations to their families and every Ramblewood resident. They'd even personally delivered invitations to Adam's parents and sister on Christmas day. Their unexpected visit caught Adam's parents off guard, but by the end of the day, they seemed to warm to Adam's new appearance and listened while he explained his plans for a music school and recording studio along with Bridgett's restaurant.

Late Christmas evening, Bridgett and Abby dropped

in on their biological father after hearing he was spending another holiday alone. They invited him to the wedding, and he thanked them but was afraid he'd overshadow their big day. They left the decision up to him.

Considering Bridgett was supposed to be Abby's maid of honor, they changed things up a bit, each couple being the other's maid of honor and best man. With only minutes to go before Ruby walked her two daughters down the aisle, Bridgett's nerves began to ramp up. Peeking out at their wedding guests, she was thrilled to see Adam's parents arrive moments before the wedding procession began.

A few months ago, Bridgett never would have imagined she'd be walking down the aisle, beside a twin sister! The fast friendship they had formed when Abby had first come to town had once again blossomed. Bridgett had always wanted a sister to confide in, and now she had one, however unexpected.

The thought of leaving town was a distant memory. As they walked down the aisle, Bridgett felt the love radiating off their guests. Almost the entire town had come, including their new half siblings and Darren. This was where she belonged. This was home.

At midnight on New Year's Eve, Abby and Bridgett stood side by side, as they pledged their love to the men in their lives. And even though they'd learned that good intentions don't always turn out as expected, they'd also discovered that the honesty in their hearts would always prevail.

* * * * *

COMING NEXT MONTH FROM

H HARLEQUIN®

American Romance®

Available June 2, 2015

SPECIAL EXCERPT FROM

H HARLEQUIN®

American Romance®

*Rose McCabe wants to use Clint McCulloch's newly
acquired ranch for blackberry farming, but the sexy
cowboy wants it for pastureland for his herd. Can the
two come to a temporary agreement?*

Read on for a sneak preview of
LONE STAR DADDY
by **Cathy Gillen Thacker**,
part of her **MCCABE MULTIPLES** *miniseries.*

"You can ignore me as long as you want. I am not going
away." Rose McCabe followed Clint McCulloch around the
big farm tractor.

Wrench in one hand, a grimy cloth in another, the rodeo
cowboy turned rancher paused to give her a hostile glare.
"Suit yourself," he muttered beneath his breath. Then went
right back to working on the engine that had clearly seen
better days.

Aware she was taking a tiger by the tail, Rose stomped
closer. "Sooner or later you're going to have to hear me out."

"Actually, I won't." Sweat glistened on the suntanned
skin of his broad shoulders and muscular back, dripped
down the strip of dark hair that covered his chest, and
arrowed down into the fly of his faded jeans.

Still ignoring her, he moved around the wheel to turn the
key in the ignition.

It clicked. But did not catch.

He strode back to the engine once more, giving Rose
a good view of his ruggedly handsome face and the thick

chestnut hair that fell onto his brow and curled damply against the nape of his neck. At six foot four, there was no doubt Clint was every bit as much as stubborn—and breathtakingly masculine—as he had been when they were growing up.

"The point is—" he said "—I'm not interested in being a berry farmer. I'm a rancher. I want to restore the Double Creek Ranch to the way it was when my dad was alive. Run cattle and breed and train cutting horses here." He pointed to the blackberry patch up for debate. "And those thorn- and weed-infested bushes are sitting on the most fertile land on the entire ranch."

Rose's expression turned pleading. "Just let me help you out."

"No." He refused to be swayed by a sweet-talking woman, no matter how persuasive and beguiling. He had gone down that road once before, with a heartbreaking result.

A silence fell and Rose blinked. "No?" she repeated, as if she were sure she had heard wrong.

"No," he reiterated flatly. His days of being seduced or pressured into anything were long over. Then he picked up his wrench. "And now, if you don't mind, I really need to get back to work…"

Don't miss LONE STAR DADDY
by Cathy Gillen Thacker,
available June 2015 wherever
Harlequin® American Romance®
books and ebooks are sold.

www.Harlequin.com